it's not you,
it's me

also by Kerry Cohen Hoffmann

The Good Girl

Easy

a *novel by* KERRY COHEN HOFFMANN

it's not you,
it's me

DELACORTE PRESS

Copyright © 2009 by Kerry Cohen Hoffmann

Visit us on the Web! www.randomhouse.com/teens

Educators and librarians, for a variety of teaching tools, visit us at www.randomhouse.com/teachers

Library of Congress Cataloging-in-Publication Data
Hoffman, Kerry Cohen.
It's not you, it's me / Kerry Cohen Hoffman. — 1st ed.
p. cm.
Summary: Follows sixteen-year-old Zoë through the first thirty-one days after Henry, her boyfriend of six months, breaks up with her, as she moves from being obsessed with getting back together to finding herself again.
ISBN 978-0-385-73696-1 (hardcover) — ISBN 978-0-385-90638-8 (library binding) — ISBN 978-0-375-89225-7 (e-book) [1. Dating (Social customs)—Fiction. 2. Identity—Fiction. 3. Self-confidence—Fiction. 4. High schools—Fiction. 5. Schools—Fiction.] I. Title.
PZ7.H67546Its 2009
[Fic]—dc22
2008031141

The text of this book is set in 12-point Sabon.

Book design by Angela Carlino

Printed in the United States of America

10 9 8 7 6 5 4 3 2 1

First Edition

Random House Children's Books supports the First Amendment and celebrates the right to read.

For all to whom it has seemed you were the only one
to have ever felt this way, and then when you were told
"There are plenty of fish in the sea" and "It's for the
best, you'll see," you knew you were right.

You don't die from a broken heart. You only wish you had.

—Anonymous

it's not you,
it's me

Day 1

Three weeks ago, Henry held Zoë's face between his hands and kissed her for the 199th time. Zoë had been keeping track. She couldn't help it. Each kiss was like a tiny revelation, an aha moment. Each kiss sent electricity down her body, snaking its way around her legs until it reached her feet. *Aha.* This kiss, though, this kiss was different. This was the kiss Henry gave her after she told him she loved him. It had begun to rain, but they stayed outside her house near the laurel bushes after one of the open-mike gigs Henry and his band played every other week. She had watched him play his guitar, his mouth moving involuntarily, his eyes closed, and she'd known it was true. She had fallen in love. This kiss was about love. She wrapped her arms around his neck and stood on her tiptoes, meeting the softness of his lips. He put his hands around her waist and lifted her off the ground, just like in the movies, just like Zoë always figured love would be. And here it was, big, soft, rainy, and all hers.

But now Zoë knows it's all over. She knows because when she called Henry at their normal time of 9 p.m., his voice mail answered. Zoë hung up, a thick feeling in her throat that hasn't gone away. She's got ten hours. Ten long hours to live through before she can leave for school and find out what's really going on.

She calls Julia and explains the situation.

"Maybe he's sick," Julia says. Zoë's aware that her right leg is bouncing a hundred miles a minute. She presses a hand against it to stop it.

"He's not sick." She doesn't know why she called Julia first. She opens her computer and checks for e-mails or IMs, but the screen is eerily empty. She opens Henry's MySpace page, and his picture, the one where he's playing guitar, pops up. She hates this picture because his head is down and his hair is in his eyes. You can barely see him. But there's no activity. She clicks the page closed.

"Maybe he was taking a shower."

"He wasn't taking a shower either, Jules."

"I don't know what you want me to say," Julia says,

obviously annoyed that Zoë's annoyed. "I'm trying to come up with explanations."

"I know," Zoë tells her. "I'm sorry." She stands and starts pacing her room, seeing the usual stuff: shoes arranged neatly by her made bed, and books stacked on her desk, waiting to be cracked for homework. "I'm freaked out."

"I can tell."

"Maybe I should call Shannon."

"You haven't called the Guru yet?" This is what they call Shannon, the Wise One concerning all matters of the heart. "Hang up this phone, fool. You called the wrong friend."

Zoë laughs. At least Julia has made her laugh. "Thanks, Jules."

She dials Shannon.

"Listen to me, Z," Shannon says once Zoë fills her in, "I want you to sit down and take a few deep breaths."

"Okay, okay," Zoë says.

"Are you doing it?"

Zoë rolls her eyes and sits heavily on the bed. She takes the breaths.

"I know you," Shannon continues. "You've already turned this into Something Meaningful. Nothing's happened. He didn't answer his phone, that's it."

"But in six months?" Zoë can hear the whine in her voice. "In six months we haven't missed a nine p.m. phone call."

"Zoë." Shannon only uses Zoë's full name when she means business. "I'm not saying things look good, but you have no proof that things are bad either."

"Maybe I can get proof," Zoë says in a measured voice.

"Zoë."

"I could go over there, just happen to be walking by."

"Zoë!"

"Or I could quickly peek in the windows. I'd only have to see Henry to know what he's feeling."

Zoë hears Shannon sigh.

"Shannon." That whine is back in her voice. She tries to tame it. "That's how well I know him. I love him. As of three weeks ago I'm officially in love."

Shannon is silent. Then she says softly, "I'm going to tell you this only once, so you need to listen." When Zoë doesn't respond, she says, "Are you listening to me?"

"Yes."

"Do not leave your house. Do not call him. Do not call anyone else. Your mission for this evening is to do your homework and go to bed like any other night. Understand?"

"I can't call him again?"

"Z, if you call him again you're going to be very sorry."

"Even to remind him I love him?"

"Especially for that."

"So I have to just sit here?"

"And do your homework."

Panic rises into Zoë's chest. "I can't stop thinking about this. I need to know if he still wants to be with me."

"No," Shannon says. "You don't. You need to continue as though it never happened."

Zoë slumps forward. "I don't know how."

"You'll figure it out," Shannon says. "Focus on homework."

Zoë groans and looks up at her books. "I don't know how to block it out," she says again.

"I have faith."

Zoë stares at the books a moment longer, clutching the phone to her ear.

"This will be good for you, Z. You need to learn how to let go. Letting go is not one of your strengths."

"I'm well aware of that."

"I love you," Shannon says. "If you have to, call me again."

When they hang up, Zoë doesn't move. She can hear her heart thudding in her chest, along with the faint buzz of her computer's fan. Her books loom malevolently on the desk. In the silence she hears her mom and dad in the kitchen. She gets up and steps out into the hallway. Their voices are gentle; she can't make out the words. It's always the same thing, though, always love and kisses. For the most part Zoë likes having parents who are so happy together, but sometimes she gets tired of hearing about it. Now, for example, when it's possible she has lost *her* love, is not a time she wants to hear them.

She tiptoes to Logan's room and makes out gruff sounds coming from his PlayStation. She also gets tired of the way her parents never seem to notice when something's not perfect, like Logan's endless video-game playing. Maybe it wouldn't be such a big deal if the characters in the game actually accomplished something meaningful, but all they do is take each other out with machine guns. Is this what a ten-year-old boy should be doing with his time? She goes back to her room and looks down at the phone still in her hand. Immediately her mind is back on Henry.

There must be some way, some small thing she can do to get relief. She takes the phone to her desk and opens drawers, looking for the school directory. Shannon, who volunteers as a peer counselor at school, would be pissed; Zoë's not listening to her at all. But Shannon doesn't know what it's like in Zoë's house—the silence from Henry, the soft voices of love downstairs. Shannon's mother has been in therapy since her divorce. It's not that Zoë wants her parents to be unhappy. She just wishes she were better prepared for potential destruction. Something's wrong with her and Henry, and she has to find out what. Just this one thing, and then she'll listen. She swears.

She finds the directory in the third drawer and flips forward to the name Niles Murray. Next to it is Niles's phone number. She checks the time: 10:30 p.m. Probably pushing it, but an emergency is an emergency.

After three rings, he picks up.

"Hey, Niles," she says, trying to sound casual.

"Who is this? Zoë?"

"Right," she says. "How's it going?"

"Okay, I guess." She's never called Niles before. He's Henry's friend, the bassist in their band—a band that consists of Henry, Niles, and the drummer, David Jefferson—but Zoë hasn't had many conversations with Niles. A cold feeling pierces her. Maybe this wasn't such a smart idea.

"I know it's kind of weird for me to call you."

"I'm not really allowed phone calls after ten." He's clearly irritated. She needs to move fast.

"I'm sorry," she says. "I have something important to tell Henry but I couldn't reach him. I thought maybe you'd know what was going on?"

Niles is silent. That cold feeling makes its way into her limbs. She swallows.

"I have no idea what Henry's doing," Niles says finally.

"Okay," she says, still trying to sound nonchalant. Her voice is shaking a little. "I'll just see you tomorrow then."

"Harrumph," he mumbles, and hangs up.

She winces.

Maybe she needs to listen to Shannon. She pulls her calculus book off the stack and opens it to page 127. *Find delta given epsilon.* Normally, doing math feels good. She loves the straightforward answers. But right now math feels the way Julia says it feels for her—like a foreign language. Zoë leaves the book open but goes to lie on her bed. That thudding is still there in her chest. Her parents' laughter rises from the kitchen. Zoë closes her eyes, trying to block it all out, trying to concentrate on Henry.

She thinks about the last time she saw Henry. She and Henry met at her locker like they always do. She told him about her Spanish quiz and he laughed when she relayed what Julia had said about Mr. Grier's new haircut. Henry kissed her when the bell rang and they went to their separate classes. Was he distant? Annoyed with her? She tries to remember the way his eyes looked, but they were bright and attentive as always. His beautiful brown eyes. She rolls over and presses her face into the pillow.

She doesn't want to lose him. After six months, the longest relationship she's ever had, really the only relationship, she can't stand the thought of him not being her boyfriend. He's the second boy she's ever kissed, the only one she's allowed to go further. She closes her eyes, thinking of his smell—sweet and musky—and the feel of his hair in her fingers. It can't be over. She's deeply in love with him. She strokes the bed, wishing he were with her. They've never had sex, but she has secretly hoped she will lose her virginity to him, when the timing is right. Now she wonders if this is doomed never to happen.

She remembers that night three weeks ago when she proclaimed her love. For the first time, she realizes he didn't say anything back. She was so swept up in the kiss, in his lifting her off the ground, she didn't pay attention. Now this little fact worms its way beneath her skin and pokes its head up into her consciousness.

She can't help herself. She sits up, gets the phone, and dials his number, knowing it by heart, of course, everything with him by heart. It rings four times, and when his voice mail answers, she pushes the Off button on the receiver.

Day 2

Logan is in the kitchen eating pancakes when Zoë comes down the next morning. Mom is visible through the doorway, sitting at the dining room table in front of her sewing machine. The machine whirs and rumbles as she runs fabric through it. A roll of red velvet unfurls on the table, its edge uneven. Scissors and fabric tape sit on top. This is Mom's new obsession. She is making curtains for the dining room windows. Last month it was canning raspberry preserves.

"Want pancakes?" Mom asks without turning to

face Zoë. She speaks through closed lips, holding pins.

Zoë looks at Logan's plate and frowns. "I don't know how you eat that so early in the morning."

Logan picks up a pancake with his hand and stuffs the whole thing into his mouth. He grins, showing her the chewed food.

"Gross," she says.

"I'll take that as a no," Mom says, her body bent in concentration as she works the machine, oblivious as always, Zoë thinks, to her sweet little boy's behavior.

Zoë goes to the refrigerator and takes out the orange juice, then reaches into the cupboard for a glass. "Where's Dad?"

"He left early for work."

"Again?" Zoë asks. Dad's a lawyer, and he's often not around; he's trying to make partner. Zoë believes most moms would be a little bit bothered by that, but hers is unfazed, as always. When it comes to Dad, it's like Mom has some kind of muffler over her body, keeping her from feeling anything but just fine. Zoë fears this is what love has to be like. Impatient and difficult as Zoë knows she is, maybe no one will ever be comfortable with all her demands, with all her nervous energy.

"Go easy on your dad, honey," Mom says. "He's—"

"Trying to make partner," Zoë finishes for her. "I know."

Mom smiles. "Is that all you're having? Orange juice?"

Zoë nods. She's too nervous to eat, too nervous to do

anything but get to school and find out what's happening with Henry.

"Some toast?"

She shakes her head. "I have to go."

"At least take a banana."

"Mom." She hates it when Mom does this, when her mother focuses all her energy on something that doesn't matter, like whether Zoë eats breakfast, or like those curtains, when clearly there are more significant considerations. Zoë glances at Logan, who was waiting for her to look. He grins, his fork hanging from his nose like some kind of tribal ornament. How does he even do that?

"Control your child," Zoë tells Mom as she grabs her bag from the chair near the door.

Mom just smiles and raises her hand in a wave. "Have a good day," she says, turning back to her sewing.

The bus hits every red light and slows for every pedestrian. Zoë taps her foot on the floor, raps her fingers on the metal back of the seat in front of her. By the time she arrives at school, she's ready to leap from her skin. It takes everything she has to walk at a reasonable pace toward her locker. One of the insults of being a junior is the placement of their lockers on the third floor, as if it isn't enough to have been going to this school for three years and still have no privileges. She climbs the stairs, her heart doing flip-flops.

When she rounds the last landing and Henry is not

there, her stomach sinks. Where is he? Every day for the past six months he's been there, waiting for her. He's a senior and is dignified with a locker on the first floor, but he still climbs those stairs every morning to meet Zoë at hers. His first class also happens to be on the third floor. Zoë walks heavily past the people in the hall to her locker and works the combination. Maybe it's time to accept that something's definitely wrong.

She unloads her books, none of which, she's aware, she did anything with last night. This will be a first— Zoë Gill with no homework to turn in. Shannon will be mad, Julia shocked. But until she gets some answers, Zoë doesn't care all that much.

She glances around the hallway. Still no sign of him. She looks at her watch. Just two minutes until class. A girl says hi. Zoë says hi back. Finally, resigned, she picks up her bag and makes her way toward Spanish. This is when she sees him coming toward her in the hall: his lumbering walk, disheveled hair, backpack strung over both shoulders. He's holding his jacket, the one he wears when there might be rain. She exhales, relieved. She can feel her whole being settle back onto Earth.

But as Henry gets closer, she sees the expression on his face, and her smile drops.

"What?" she says when he's still a good ten feet away. "What's going on?"

"Nothing," he says. He's smiling, but it's his polite smile, the one he gives people when he's uncomfortable.

He doesn't kiss her. She touches his arm, but she feels him flinch.

"I knew it," she says.

"You knew what?"

"You're breaking up with me."

This, of all times, is when the bell rings. Lockers slam. People rush past them, a sea of jeans and back-packs and hair product.

"Meet me at the Big Top after school," he says. "We need to talk."

And then he walks away.

• • •

"That can't be good," Julia says.

They're at lunch, outside because it didn't wind up raining. Julia, Shannon, and Zoë sit on the brick ledge facing the street. The air smells of new grass and fresh earth. At the edge of the lawn the small trees are budding.

"You're not helping," Shannon tells Julia.

"She's right," Zoë says. " 'We need to talk' is a breakup line." She stares hopelessly at her sandwich. Why, she wonders, did she buy a sandwich when she knew she wasn't going to eat?

"If it is a breakup, which we don't know for sure yet," Shannon says, looking at Zoë meaningfully, "you need to prepare yourself."

Julia reaches up to scratch her short platinum hair. "I

don't see how preparing herself is going to make a difference. If he's dumping her he's dumping her."

"Julia, please." Shannon shoots her a look. "I'm talking about preserving her dignity."

Julia shakes her head and looks at Zoë. Her big eyes are lined with black makeup. "I don't see what the big deal is. We're sixteen. It's not like you were going to get married."

Zoë looks down. A car rumbles by. It bounces over the small pothole that's been out in front of the school for years.

"Oh, no," Julia says. "You thought you were going to marry this guy?"

"I hadn't completely canceled out the possibility."

Shannon laughs. A few girls sitting on a nearby wooden bench glance over, and Zoë gives Shannon a look to keep it down.

"Come on," Zoë says softly. "If there's a girl out there who claims she hasn't strung her first name with a boy's last name, she's lying."

Shannon looks off, thinking about this. A gust of wind shakes her dark curls. "I was Shannon Tiernan for a week last year," she admits.

"Will?" Julia stares at Shannon with shock on her pale face. "You liked Will Tiernan?"

"Did any girl not like Will Tiernan?"

Julia raises her hand.

"Julia doesn't like boys yet," Zoë tells Shannon, referring to the many guys Julia's turned down.

Julia scoffs. "I like boys. Not idiot boys," she says as

she takes a sip from her Pepsi, which she drinks all day, every day. Never Diet Pepsi, she makes a point of letting people know. Diet drinks, she says, are for Barbies, the kind of girl she plans never to be. "Just because I don't let boys take over my whole life doesn't mean I don't like them."

"That's true." Shannon looks pointedly at Zoë.

"I don't let boys take over my life." Even as Zoë says it, she knows she's a liar. She knows Shannon and Julia are probably thinking of the book club she used to be a part of before Henry. She dropped that book club two months into Henry-land. Or they're thinking of the dance class she took with Julia, a class that Julia has now advanced in but Zoë has left behind, even though Henry said he thought it was sexy that she danced. Or maybe they've got the school literary magazine on their minds—the one Zoë launched back in September. Zoë doesn't meet Julia's eyes, but she can picture the indignation on her friend's face.

"No," Julia says. "Only Henry for the past four months."

"Six," Zoë says.

"Whatever."

Zoë presses her lips tight to keep from saying how significant it is that it was six months. It wouldn't be well received.

"You've been spending all your time with him," Shannon says now. "Maybe some space between you would be good."

Zoë frowns, pressing little holes into her sandwich with her finger.

"You could focus on yourself for a while," Shannon continues. "And your friends." She raises her eyebrows.

"Hos over bros," Julia adds.

"Okay," Zoë says. "Conversation over."

They jump down from the ledge and gather up their garbage. But Zoë doesn't miss the look Shannon and Julia exchange.

• • •

Henry's already sitting at their table when Zoë arrives at the Big Top. He's looking down, his hands grasping and releasing each other over and over again on his lap. Zoë's heart jumps around in her chest. Lead sits in her belly. She feels so sick, she's afraid she'll have to rush to the bathroom. She stands inside the doorway, not wanting to go in, not wanting time to move forward to the inevitable. Maybe she can just stay like this, she thinks, a girl going to meet her boyfriend at their café, where they've shared good times and laughs. Where they've held hands and kissed, not caring what others thought. Maybe things don't have to change.

But Henry sees her, and with that same polite smile as before he waves her over.

Zoë goes and sits across from him, watching his face. He won't meet her eyes.

"Just say it," she says. Her heart is already in a hundred pieces.

"Zoë." He still doesn't look at her.

"Say it," she says again.

"It has nothing to do with you."

Her face feels like a statue, hard and unmoving. She watches his hands, still gripping and opening like he doesn't know how to stop them.

"I don't want a girlfriend right now."

Zoë remains silent.

"I'm a teenager. I want to do other stuff. I want to focus on the band."

Finally his eyes meet hers. They look pained and also concerned. Zoë's not sure what he sees in her expression. His nose, the nose that's bumped hers before kissing, wrinkles.

"I know you want to say something," he says.

Her jaw feels tight. She's afraid if she says just one thing everything else will spill out. That she loves him, that she hates him, that she doesn't want this to be happening. She notices music tinkling from the speakers in the ceiling. She thinks of what Shannon said about dignity and takes a measured breath. "Fine," she says. It comes out as a squeak.

"Really?" He looks relieved. Her stomach grows hollow, yawning open like a cavern. "I just think it's best. We've been together a long time. We had a lot of fun. But I've got nearly three more months of senior year and you have another year and a half. We should be free for that."

Zoë watches him, her face still stonelike.

"I care about you, Zoë. I do. I hope we'll stay friends. I know that's such a cliché, but I really mean it. You're a cool girl."

She nods once.

"Great. I knew it. I knew you'd be cool. I mean, I didn't think you'd be this cool, but I had my hopes." He laughs a little, a short, nervous laugh. Did he always talk this much? she wonders vaguely. It's hard to believe that this is the same boy who seemed to love her, whom she'd set her hopes on for the future. "So." He releases his hands for good now. She tries not to look at them, at those fingers that used to weave through hers, the freckle on his left hand that she's kissed. "I guess I'll see you around."

He gets up, so Zoë does too. They stand there a moment, facing each other, their arms at their sides as though awaiting instructions. He steps forward to hug her, but she backs away, on instinct. A hug would be too painful, too awful to bear. She'd have to inhale his scent, feel the weight of him, the hardness of his chest. It would be too much. All of this, too much. She takes another step back. Then she turns and runs, not wanting him to see her cry.

• • •

The Big Top is a nice long walk from home, which is exactly what Zoë wants. She strides forward, letting the rhythmic movement settle over her. She doesn't want to think about what just happened or what she's supposed to do now. She focuses instead on the budding oaks, the crocuses peeking out from the newly softened ground, the pink petals just beginning to show themselves on the dogwood trees. How is it that everything around her is opening and loosening, when inside all she feels is numb? She moves fast, listening to her breath, which comes quickly from the exertion. Six long months, and now this. It seems impossible, and yet it is.

Uncontrollably, a memory comes. Early January, a couple of months ago. The air was unseasonably warm, up in the fifties somewhere. She and Henry walked hand in hand along the Willamette. A strong breeze rose off the water, making their hair whip around. They laughed. He was talking about his band, Spaghetti Carbonara. The week before, the band had performed at some girls' party, and now three more people had booked them to play.

"I can't freaking believe this is really happening," he said. "We're finally getting noticed."

"But you guys rock," Zoë told him, always careful to be encouraging.

"You think?"

"I know. I'm at every rehearsal."

He grew quiet, looking out at the water. A couple of seagulls squawked and soared overhead.

"What?" she said. "Something's wrong."

"No," he said. He looked at his Vans, at those sea-gulls, anywhere but at her.

"Just tell me," Zoë said.

"It's just the guys." He let go of her hand to run his own through his hair. The wind was awfully annoying, Zoë noticed. "They made a Yoko Ono joke."

"They think I'm being a Yoko?" Zoë's voice rose defensively.

"No, no." He walked forward, his hands stuffed in his pockets. To Zoë he suddenly seemed far away. "They were just commenting on you being at rehearsals all the time, that's all."

"I'm supporting you."

"Totally."

"Besides, I'm not at *every* rehearsal. I missed that one a few weeks ago."

"Sure." He laughs, like she's being ridiculous.

"And it's not like I'm trying to tell you guys what to play. That's what Yoko Ono did."

"Absolutely."

Zoë set her mouth, frustrated and embarrassed that his friends would see her this way. "What did you say to them?"

He shrugged. "I don't want to make a big deal out of it."

"What did you say, though?"

"I guess I told them I'd talk to you about coming less."

"You did?" Zoë felt sick to her stomach.

Henry shrugged again.

"Why didn't you tell me?"

"I just did. But it's not a big deal. Could we drop it?"

"I don't want to drop it," she said, though this wasn't entirely true. She was embarrassed to talk about the fact that his bandmates wanted her gone, but she was hurt too. She wanted him to say something kind and comforting. She wanted him to have defended her.

"Well, I do," he said. He kept walking, shoulders hunched, hands still submerged in his pockets. She knew this posture. It was his conversation-over stance, and there was no penetrating that wall. So she swallowed down her hurt and trudged forward beside him.

But now she thinks maybe this was it. Maybe this was when he began to think of ending things. She wishes she could go back, find the right balance between attending rehearsals and not attending them. She wishes she had spent more time determining how to be the perfect girlfriend.

As Zoë approaches her house she sees her mother through the bay window, still at the dining room table. Mom is seated at the sewing machine, but she's not sewing. She's looking out the window, a dreamy expression on her face. Zoë braces herself. Everything for Mom is contentedness. And then here is Zoë, wracked and ruined. She feels terribly, awfully alone.

Inside, Logan is stomping around the kitchen, circling the island, singing something obnoxious and loud. Zoë looks from him to Mom, then back to him.

"Are you on drugs?" Zoë asks, loudly so he'll hear her over his singing.

Mom startles and turns to see her. "You're home," she says.

"Are *you* on drugs?" Logan says.

Zoë sneers, but he ignores her. For the first time ever, she wants him to argue with her. She needs the distraction. She needs something other than this pit in her stomach. She grips the edge of the counter, focusing her energy on the solidness of it. She waits for Mom to notice that something's wrong, but the sewing machine starts whirring.

"Mom," Zoë says.

"Hmmm?"

"Mom," she says more loudly. Logan's song reaches a crescendo; then he begins it again.

"What is it, Zoë?" Mom says. She turns around finally and looks at Zoë.

Tears sting Zoë's eyes. "Henry broke up with me," she blurts out.

"Oh, honey," Mom says, standing and coming over. She hugs Zoë. "I'm so sorry."

Logan sings loudly, stomping some more as he passes by them.

"I don't even understand why."

"We can't always know the reasons people do the things they do," Mom says, stroking Zoë's hair.

"But I should," Zoë says. "It was my relationship too."

"Sometimes we just have to accept what happens."

Zoë pulls away. She's irritated. Maybe because Logan's still yelling, because Mom hasn't made him stop. "Why should I?" Zoë says. "Why should I accept it?"

She feels Mom's eyes on her as she runs from the room. Even Logan, still singing, stops to watch. Mom can't understand, Zoë thinks. She takes things as they come, and still she's happy. But Zoë's different. She needs things to be a certain way to be happy. Mainly, she needs Henry. It was true what she said: It was her relationship too, and if she doesn't want it to be over, she doesn't have to let it be. She'll fight to get him back. She'll be the perfect girlfriend.

She gets to her room, closes the door behind her, and sits at her desk. Every teen movie ever made follows the same scenario—girl loves boy, boy leaves girl, girl proves her love and gets boy back. There's no reason she can't get her boy back too. Her legs are tired. Her head aches. Her eyes feel swollen from crying. But her heart, her heart has a glimmer of hope.

Day 3

Zoë crouches down behind a row of bushes outside Henry's house. She's acutely aware of how mad Shannon would be right now. But she pushes this from her mind and focuses on what's in front of her. Namely, a house with too many windows through which people might see her.

She pulls a piece of paper from her pocket. On it she's written a poem for Henry.

> *Lying here without you*
> *All I want to do is sleep,*

*To turn off the world that somehow
has to keep spinning without you.*

Her throat tightens with longing.

*But I can't close my eyes.
Behind them is you.
Eyes open, I'm with you.
Eyes closed, I'm with you.
You won't leave me alone
—no matter how you try.*

Tears pierce her eyes for the millionth time. She has to get through to him. She has to make him understand what a mistake he's made.

She puts the paper back in her pocket and crawls out from behind the bushes into Henry's front yard. The smell of the grass is strong. Above her, the night sky is sparkly. A wispy cloud floats in front of the moon. Last time she was here was on an evening much like tonight, only she was walking, not crawling, and she was holding Henry's hand. They had returned from dinner out with his parents, and she and Henry were lingering on the porch. She looked up at the stars, thinking about something as insignificant as laundry or a quiz problem she'd gotten wrong. The insignificant things she had the luxury of thinking about before every single thought had to be of Henry and how he is no longer hers. That night, before they went inside, Henry leaned down and brushed Zoë's lips with his, something they have done a total of 218 times. Zoë craves those kisses. She wishes she hadn't just counted each kiss, but had bottled every single one so she could shake them out, one by one, savoring their sweetness on her mouth.

She remembers they'd been discussing the future, how Henry would be going off to the University of Oregon in the fall. It felt sad, but his departure also seemed a long way off, and she assumed they would have all of the spring and summer together. When she imagined the future, she pictured herself visiting him at school, walking hand in hand through the tree-lined campus she saw in his brochures.

"I can't wait to go," Henry said.

"How can you say that?" Zoë looked up at him, bewildered. "You're leaving me."

He laughed dismissively. "I'm also heading toward something."

Zoë looked down at her hands, silent. Henry pulled her into his arms.

"You'll visit me."

"Promise?"

"Sure," he said. "Why not?"

"You won't forget about me?"

Henry sighed, still holding her. "Come on, Zo. You're being crazy."

She bit her lip. She knew he hated it when she got all clingy, but she couldn't help it. She couldn't stand the thought of being without him, even then.

"You're my girl," he told her.

She leaned her head back and kissed him. "I love it when you call me your girl."

"My girl," he said again. He started crooning. " 'My girl, talking 'bout my girl, my girl.' "

She laughed. He laughed. They kissed again. And everything was fine.

She closes her eyes now as she crawls closer to the house, trying to push aside all these terrible, wonderful memories. How will she ever be free of them? Six months of memories. It pains her to think he doesn't feel the same, that he's in this house, just a few yards from her. His chest doesn't feel some great weight. He feels, like he said the other day, talking like someone she barely knew, free. Freed of her. She can't stand to think of it.

I want to focus on the band, he said. She reaches the base of the maple tree whose branches stretch above the house. She stands. She raises a foot and nestles it in a crook of the tree. The whole tree shakes and she freezes, listening to see if anyone has heard. Is she really doing this, climbing Henry's tree?

His band—Spaghetti Carbonara. She hates that band. Not because of the music. The music was actually good to listen to, all those afternoons she spent sitting in Niles's garage while they practiced. She hates Spaghetti Carbonara because it was often all Henry seemed interested in. He could be so singularly focused, as if she weren't right there while he noodled around on his guitar.

Now, though, on the fourth branch up the tree, she wonders if he could feel her insincerity when it came to his band. The truth is she often wanted to be doing something else, like participating in the book club or preparing to attend the spring break Shakespeare camp in Ashland. She'd done that the year before, but threw out the brochure when it arrived last fall. She didn't want to spend her entire spring break away from Henry.

An issue of *Glamour* she read in her dentist's waiting room said that to keep a man's attention you had to get involved in his interests. She thought that was what she was doing, but maybe it was just a facade. Even with his bandmates calling her a Yoko Ono, maybe Zoë wasn't involved enough. Or maybe her involvement was really a smokescreen for wanting him near her at all costs. Maybe it had nothing to do with his interests.

As she steps up to the next branch, the one beneath breaks off with a sharp *crick!* Zoë freezes again, her heart pounding. No, Shannon would definitely not approve. Above her Zoë can see the light on in Henry's room. He must be in there, carrying on with his life, his life without her. She climbs higher, just a few branches now from his window. The tree sways from her weight. She realizes she might fall. She glances down, seeing the dark ground far below, and catches her breath. She can picture Julia, shaking her head: *I don't let boys take over my life.* Zoë's aware that her current position, ten feet up a tree outside Henry's house, doesn't make her look good. But this is Henry. They had something real together. For all Julia's adamant opinions about boys, she has no grounding for them. She's never had a boyfriend. Unless you count her relationship with Seth Jessup back in sixth grade. As far as Zoë knows, Seth's the only boy Julia's kissed. This most definitely makes her no expert on how Zoë should be feeling now that Henry's ripped out her heart and torn it to shreds.

Julia doesn't know what it's like. No one knows.

Zoë nestles her foot on the next branch. Then she is there, just under Henry's window. Muted light comes through his shade. She cranes her neck and sees that she's in luck. On this beautiful night he's opened his window just a touch. She reaches behind her and slides the poem from her pocket, then pushes it through the gap. Her heart picks up its pace again. She stays still, listening. Part of her hopes he will come to the window, throw it open, and respond like the lover in "Rapunzel" or like Romeo. But another part of her, a darker part, a scolding part, imagines that she looks nothing like a damsel in love but rather like someone deranged by grief. And this part is terrified he'll see her, hanging like a fool from his tree.

Voices. Zoë freezes and looks down, where a woman is saying good-bye at the front door. Zoë hears Henry's mother's voice.

"Yes," Henry's mother says. "I will. Drive safely now. We'll see you soon."

The door closes, and the woman makes her way across the long front walkway. This is when the bough beneath Zoë decides to give out. Her leg scrapes against the bark, and she grasps desperately at the branches. In the turmoil, and in her attempt to grip the tree trunk, she scratches her cheek on a twig. The scrape stings. Her arms are wrapped around the tree. Her breath comes quickly and heavily, as does her heartbeat. But somehow she is not lying unconscious on the ground.

"I see you," the woman calls up to her. "And I'm calling the police." In the moonlight, Zoë can make out a woman wearing a down vest and a scarf, overdressed for this beautiful spring night.

"No," Zoë whispers loudly. She scrambles as fast as she can down the tree. "I'm Henry's girlfriend." That cavern inside yawns open again. She's not Henry's girl-friend, not anymore. "His friend," she corrects. She reaches the ground, and the woman peers at her.

"You're bleeding." The woman looks concerned now.

"I am?"

"If you're Henry's girlfriend, why are you out here climbing this tree?"

Zoë puts her hand up to her cheek, which is stinging terribly. She can feel the blood there. She looks at the woman, unsure what to say.

"Maybe I should get Mrs. Bole," the woman says.

Before Zoë can say no, the front door opens, and Henry's mother, Mrs. Bole, steps out.

"Zoë?"

"Oh, god," Zoë says, panicking.

"What's going on out here?"

Mrs. Bole's friend puts her hands on her hips and looks at Zoë, waiting for her to explain.

"I'm sorry," Zoë says, stepping backward. "I made a mistake. I'm just going to go."

"Hold on a moment." Mrs. Bole starts walking toward them.

Zoë's heart stops. It takes everything in her not to set off running. She's certain Mrs. Bole must be angry and wondering what she's up to. If there were a hole anywhere nearby Zoë would jump straight into it.

Zoë's sure she's going to be reprimanded, and that Henry will look out his window to see what all the ruckus is. And her leaving the poem—which seemed like such a simple, passionate, brilliant idea—will be ruined. He won't see that she loves him. He'll only think she's lost her mind.

"Now you're going to get it," the woman mumbles to Zoë. Zoë glances at her, speechless. She didn't know grown women spoke like this.

"Sandra, will you leave us alone?" Mrs. Bole says to her friend. "It's all right, I know this girl."

"Really," Sandra says, looking intrigued. "Call me later." She turns to go to her car.

Zoë bites her lip. Her cheek is throbbing from the cut.

"I'm sorry," she says again, too embarrassed to meet Mrs. Bole's eyes.

"Zoë, honey." Something in Mrs. Bole's voice makes Zoë look up at her. "It's perfectly normal to be upset."

Zoë blinks.

"When Henry told me you were completely fine, I wondered. Now I see I was right."

"Oh." Zoë bites harder on her lip. Her mortification is thick and ugly, covering her like the dirt and twigs on her clothes. She doesn't know what makes her want to die more, losing Henry or having his mother talk to her about it.

"Go home, honey." Mrs. Bole holds back Zoë's hair with a warm hand to examine the cut. "Take care of yourself. Give yourself some time."

Zoë nods once. "Okay," she says. She walks away, wishing she could drop off the earth, evaporate into the ether. She never wants to face Mrs. Bole again.

Not only is she mortified and in physical pain, but worst of all, she still feels heartbroken.

Day 4

The next morning a yellow sticky beckons from Zoë's locker like a jewel. It's a note, from Henry! Zoë's sure of it, because of her poem. She makes her way toward it, her steps light for the first time since D-Day, Dumping Day, since Henry dug out her heart and stomped it black and blue. But when she gets there, her body turns to lead again. It's not from Henry. It's Shannon's writing.

If he says it's over, it's really over.

Zoë's face heats up. She tears the note off the locker and crumples it in her hand. She looks around, noticing a couple of kids glancing at her, curious. Zoë's so en-raged she could scream. Why would Shannon do such a mean-spirited thing—especially now when Zoë's al-ready in so much pain?

"You okay?" a girl with glittery eye shadow asks. Zoë recognizes her from calculus.

"I'm fine," Zoë says, irate. "I know what I'm doing."

The girl stares. "I mean your cheek. That looks pretty bad."

Zoë's hand flies to her cheek. Of course, her scrape. She feels the heat rise to her face again. "Right. I'm fine."

The girl looks at her oddly. "Cool," she says, and walks off.

Zoë closes her eyes. She's going to kill Shannon.

She finds Shannon outside her first-period class.

"I knew you'd come looking for me," Shannon says.

"I thought you were my friend," Zoë says.

"I'm trying to save you from yourself." Shannon frowns as a couple of kids jostle them to get into the classroom. "That's the best kind of friend there is. I needed to send you a reality check. Henry told Greg, who told Cory, who told Julia, that you somehow slipped a note into his bedroom last night."

"It was a poem," Zoë says.

"He found it on his bedroom floor."

"A poem I wrote to explain how I feel." Zoë tries to make her understand.

"That's not the point, Z," Shannon says, holding

Zoë's shoulders. "What were you doing creeping around his bedroom? Did you sneak into his house?"

"I didn't sneak into his house!"

"Then how did the poem get there?"

Mr. Brown, the economics teacher, appears at the door. "Shannon, will you be joining us today?" he asks. Zoë knows Mr. Brown. She had him last year for global history.

"I'll be right there," Shannon says, her hands still on Zoë. She searches Zoë's face, waiting for an answer.

Zoë looks down, avoiding Shannon's eyes. She doubts that telling Shannon she climbed the maple tree outside Henry's house will go over much better than if she *had* snuck into his house.

"And you have this wound on your face. What's that about?"

"Shannon." The teacher hasn't budged.

"One more minute," Shannon says to him.

"One more minute and I send you to the office for a late pass," he says. "And where are you supposed to be, Zoë?"

"Spanish."

"Then get going."

Shannon looks at Zoë one last time but releases her, and Zoë shrugs.

"We'll talk about this later," Shannon says as she turns to go into the classroom. "Unless you want another yellow sticky."

Zoë frowns and heads down the hall to the office because now she's the one who needs a late pass.

When she gets to the office, the girl with the sparkly eyelids is there. Zoë notices she also has sparkles in her long blond hair. The secretary is busily clicking away at her computer. Zoë avoids making eye contact with the girl as she moves past her.

"I need a late pass," Zoë says in a monotone.

The secretary stops clicking and looks up. She stares.

"A late pass?" Zoë says again. Did the woman not hear? Then Zoë understands. "I fell," she says.

The secretary nods, looking unconvinced. Zoë looks back at the sparkly-eyed girl, who is watching her.

"I fell," Zoë says more loudly. "Nobody's ever seen a freaking scratch on someone's face before?"

The girl looks away, her eyes wide. She thinks Zoë's crazy, Zoë's sure. Everyone thinks she's crazy. But she really doesn't care anymore.

"Can I get that pass?" She holds her hand out to the secretary, who narrows her eyes.

"Reason for being late?" the secretary asks.

Zoë eyes her back the same way. "I was bleeding." She covers her cheek with her hand and for effect adds, "Ow."

The secretary barely smiles, then scribbles her initials on a pass and hands it to Zoë.

• • •

In second-period English lit, Zoë feels another poem coming on.

I found your flannel shirt today,
Crumpled and forgotten in the bottom of my hamper.
I placed it in my bed, wishing you were there to fill it up,
To fill me up.
Like your shirt, I'm empty without you.

A folded note lands on the poem. Zoë looks back and sees Julia smirking. The note says, *What's with the facial decoration?* Zoë scribbles in big letters, *I FELL!!!* and throws the note back to Julia. She gives her friend a look to make sure Julia knows she doesn't feel like talking about it.

"Zoë," Ms. Carter says. "I hope everything's okay over there."

Zoë smiles sweetly at her. "Everything's perfect."

"Let me know." Ms. Carter, who Julia says has not had a haircut since 1982, not because of the style but because of how long and tattered it is, eyes Zoë a few beats longer before going back to discussing nature in Blake and Wordsworth. Zoë cringes. She's usually a star student. She hasn't even done the reading yet.

After class, Ms. Carter calls Zoë over.

"I hope you'll think of me as a friend," she says. Ms. Carter is one of those teachers who wants everyone to think of her as a buddy. Zoë and Julia have laughed about this before. There's one every school year. And Ms. Carter is an especially embarrassing brand of teacher-buddy because she tends to talk as though she's speaking in verse. But now Zoë considers whether Ms.

Carter *could* be a friend. She heard that Ms. Carter got divorced, only to remarry her ex. Surely she would understand what Zoë is after.

"That would be nice," Zoë says hesitantly. She drops her heavy backpack on the floor. "I could use one right now."

"Tell me." Ms. Carter comes around to the front of her desk and sits on it, clearly excited that a student has finally taken her up on her offer for friendship.

"You'll give me a late pass for my next class?"

"Absolutely."

Kids are already filing into the classroom, so Zoë talks quickly. "My boyfriend broke up with me," she says.

Ms. Carter makes a pity face.

"But I'm pretty sure it was a mistake."

Ms. Carter nods, the pity face changing to concern.

"I need to find a way to make him see."

"You have quite a dilemma." Ms. Carter pauses, and Zoë waits eagerly, hoping for words of wisdom. "If it's meant to be," Ms. Carter continues, "he'll come back to you."

"That's it?" Zoë was expecting one of her teacher's long monologues.

"That's it."

Zoë frowns. "But when you and your husband broke up, that was a mistake. You're back with him now."

Ms. Carter laughs. "I guess the private lives of faculty aren't so private."

"Isn't my situation the same?"

The teacher smiles. "It wasn't a mistake to have divorced. We came back to each other after many years, after we'd both changed in ways we needed."

"I wrote Henry a poem, though," Zoë says, hoping to appeal to Ms. Carter's literary side.

"Good for you," Ms. Carter says. "Putting your feelings into writing is healing. But you don't need to show it to him."

Zoë frowns again. She's getting tired of people telling her not to go after what she wants. Isn't that the opposite of what everyone usually encourages you to do? Go after your dreams? Follow your ambition?

"Let life unfold, Zoë," Ms. Carter says. She leans down and scribbles on a late pass and hands it to Zoë. She winks, clearly satisfied with herself.

"Thanks," Zoë says. *Thanks a whole hell of a lot* is what she thinks.

· · ·

Zoë walks quickly along the hallway. She hears muffled laughter through a classroom doorway, and then a teacher's voice. She knows she has to move fast if she doesn't want anyone to see. Henry's locker is on the far end, third from last. She knows his combination—25, 4, 7—as well as his phone number, cell, e-mail, e-mail password, and IM tag. She knows he wears a size 9 shoe and likes his T-shirts large. He uses Fructis shampoo but Pantene conditioner. His favorite color is green. He loves rock, but every once in a while he likes a country song. She knows that when asked to think of a number between 1 and 10, he will almost invariably pick 7. These little things are the ones that feel impossible to get past.

At his locker Zoë slips her latest poem through the slats, then races back to class.

Day 5

Before first period, Sam calls to her from across the hall. Sam has had a crush on Zoë since eighth grade. Everyone knows. He's made no secret of it. When they first started dating, Henry once told her, "Is it possible to not have a crush on you?" Zoë closes her eyes, remembering how he said that. She never took Sam's crush seriously, though, because Sam is a bona fide geek. He wears shorts in below-freezing weather. He talks excessively about the Mesozoic era and anything concerning dinosaurs. He listens to classical music on his iPod.

Julia has had her share of fun teasing Zoë about it. She has suggested Zoë go on a date with him, just for the story to tell later. But Zoë isn't quite that mean. Besides, Sam is a real friend. Sam worked on the school literary magazine Zoë helped launch, and not just because he liked her. They share a genuine interest in writing. She waits for Sam to catch up with her.

"Is it true?" he asks.

Zoë knows what's coming. "What did you hear?"

"That you're a single woman."

Zoë groans. "Hopefully not for long."

"That's what I'm hoping too." Sam grins.

"Keep it in your pants," Zoë says as they start walking. "I mean I'm planning to get him back."

"You are?" Sam raises his eyebrows, surprised.

Zoë nods. When Sam doesn't say anything, Zoë starts to wonder. "Why?"

"I always thought you two were sort of an odd couple."

"Really?"

"Henry hangs out with the stoners. That's not your thing. At least I hope not."

"No," Zoë says, "but it's not his thing either. They're his friends because they're into music."

Sam shrugs. "I always thought you could do better."

Zoë laughs. "Like you?"

Now Sam looks hurt. "We have more in common than you and Henry."

Zoë frowns. She doesn't want to hurt Sam's feelings,

but she also can't stand the idea of being with him *that* way. She makes a mental inventory of his interests—dinosaurs and classical music—and, with relief, honestly can't imagine what he's talking about.

"We both like good fiction," he says as if he has read her mind.

Zoë is the one to shrug now. "Lots of people like good fiction," she says, still treading carefully with his feelings. "It doesn't mean I should date them all."

"You don't have a special connection with those people," Sam says.

"And I do with *you*?"

"You know it, baby." Sam winks, and Zoë laughs.

"Give it up, Sam," she says as she goes into her classroom. She sits at her desk, thankful to have had a moment of laughter. She doesn't think she's laughed since the H-bomb.

• • •

At home that night, Zoë lays out photos on her floor. Each one is like a stab in her chest. Henry and her in Niles's garage, their smiles huge. Henry playing guitar, unaware he's being photographed. The two of them again on the school grass, Henry leaning back on his hands, his T-shirt taut against his chest. Next are the souvenirs. A ticket stub from the Harry Potter movie, which they both loved. A matchbook from the Heathman, where Henry's parents took them for dinner.

Two of Henry's guitar picks, which he said had lost their magic. She takes it all in, the tears coming again, and opens a pad of construction paper. How could he not see what they had together?

Using a glue stick, Zoë pastes pictures onto the paper and writes beneath each one. *Henry and Zoë at the beach* or *Henry playing guitar*. She draws two hearts above the picture of them on the beach and writes *H* in one, *Z* in the other. That picture was taken the day Henry kissed her for the first time. They had hung out only a couple of times before. But this was the day the upperclassmen went on a fall picnic to the beach. She and Henry played Frisbee with Shannon and a couple of Henry's friends, and then they went walking on their own.

The cold waves scrambled up the sand to their bare feet, and he laughed, pushing her toward the water as she screamed. She pushed back, feeling the warm pressure of his chest against her hands. He took her hands and pulled her close, and suddenly they were kissing, his lips soft and firm and surprising against hers. She wrapped her arms around his neck and felt his hands moving across her back. When they came apart, he smiled, and she felt light and pretty. She felt like she could run the length of the beach and back and not feel winded. Love is like that, she realizes now. It's a drug that gives you strength. Without it she feels as limp as the seaweed they saw clustered on the shore.

A knock comes at the door.

"It's almost midnight," Dad says, cracking open the door. He's in work pants and a loosened tie. "What are you still doing up?"

Zoë tries to be cheerful. "I'm working on something. I'll go to bed soon, I promise."

Dad comes closer and peers at what she's doing. "An art project?"

"Something like that." She's embarrassed to have him observe her hovering over a collage she's making for her boyfriend, ex-boyfriend, whom she's determined to get back. The desperation she feels is not what a daughter wants her father to be witness to.

She sees him recognize the pictures of Henry. "Mom told me things didn't work out between you two. I'm sorry, bunny."

Zoë tries not to meet his eyes. She doesn't want to start crying again. Why does Mom have to tell him absolutely everything? "Don't be sorry yet," she says. "I'm going to get Henry back."

Dad shuffles his feet, obviously trying to think of what he wants to say. As a lawyer, he always chooses his words carefully. "Mom told me that was your intention."

Zoë is quiet, waiting. She can tell he has more to say.

"I once prosecuted a case where a man thought he and his ex-wife were thinking alike but in fact she wanted a restraining order."

"I'm not a stalker, Dad!"

"I'm not suggesting you are. Just make sure Henry

46

wants what you want." Dad's face looks sallow and drawn, like he's been working too much and sleeping too little. Zoë wishes he and Mom would just focus on their own lives and leave her to her pining.

She examines the collage. She knows what Henry wants. He wants to concentrate on his band. He wants to be free. But isn't it possible he'll come around? That he'll realize he took Zoë for granted? It happens constantly in songs and movies. There's a girl in Zoë's grade who has broken up three times with her boyfriend, yet they keep coming back together. It happens. Why couldn't it happen with her and Henry too?

"I know what I'm doing," Zoë says. "You don't have to worry."

Dad leans down to kiss Zoë on the head. "I'm always going to worry, bunny. Even when you're thirty."

"That's stupid," Zoë says.

"Probably, but it's what parents do. Now get to bed."

"I will," Zoë says, knowing she won't. Not until she finishes the collage.

Day 6

Collage in hand, Zoë heads down the hallway toward the third-from-last locker.

She freezes.

Henry is there. Henry, whom she hasn't seen since D-Day. He's emptying books into his bag, the black messenger bag with his MUSIC ROCKS ME pin, talking to David Jefferson, Spaghetti Carbonara's drummer. Henry laughs and talks animatedly. The cavern inside Zoë opens just a little more. How can he be so happy? How, when parts of Zoë are shriveling up and dying one by one each day?

She is not sure what to do. Should she stride forward, a smile on her face, and hand him the collage like it ain't no thang? Should she crumple to the floor where he'll be sure to notice her? She's not sure. Worse, all she *can* do is stand there, her feet bolted to the ground. Henry throws his bag over his shoulder, and he and David, still talking, walk in her direction. Some guy in a Clash T-shirt bumps past her.

"Sorry," the guy says.

This is when Henry spots her. She watches as his expression changes, from contentment to confusion to concern. She blinks once, twice, and then he is right in front of her.

"Hi," he says, and keeps walking. He keeps walking— as though he never listened to intimate details of her life. As though he never confided that he was worried about his older brother in college, who he thought might be depressed. As though he never touched her in ways she would never let someone touch her if she thought one day he would just walk past her. Anger flares onto her face. She can feel it, red and warm and lifelike, the most invigorating thing she's felt since that day.

"Henry!" she calls after him. He stops and turns around. She sees his expression as she strides toward him. He's a little bit afraid. The anecdote Dad told her last night comes to mind, the one about the restraining order, but she pushes it away. She shoves the collage into Henry's hands and walks on. A few people have turned to see what's happening, their eyes wide with excitement at the possibility of drama at Lincoln High. Zoë doesn't care. Her heart hurts too much for anything else to matter.

• • •

In English lit, when they're supposed to be reading quietly, Julia throws another note onto Zoë's desk.

I'm worried about you.

Zoë turns to look at her friend and shakes her head. "Don't be," she mouths. Julia widens her eyes, writes another note, and throws it. This one lands near Zoë's shoe. Zoë glances at Ms. Carter, who is engrossed in her own reading. Zoë opens the paper.

Shannon's worried too. Why won't you talk to us?

Zoë writes below this.

I'm not NOT talking to you. I've just been busy.

Julia responds.

That's crap and you know it. We're your friends, Zoë. Talk to us.

The truth is, Zoë has been avoiding them. She knows she has. But it's not because she doesn't love them. She's avoiding them because, never having been in love, they won't understand, and being with people who don't understand is worse than being alone with her grief.

She writes, *Give me some time.*

She watches Julia read this, and when Julia looks up Zoë smiles at her. Julia smiles back. She writes one more thing and sends it to Zoë.

I'll think about it.

• • •

Lunchtime. Zoë hates lunchtime. At least during class periods she has a fair chance of thinking about something else. She can try her hardest to care about conjugating *trabajar,* or the storming of the Bastille, or whether x and y are on coordinating points. But at lunchtime she is left with only her thoughts and, normally, her friends, whom she is currently busy dodging.

She walks past the cafeteria, certain that Shannon and Julia are wondering where she is, and heads toward the gymnasium, her steps echoing in the hall. She knows this is not a good idea. After the collage incident she should probably let things lie for a few days, even for one day, but she can't. She has to do something, and as wrong as it may be, taking action offers her relief.

She rounds a corner and pulls the latest poem from her pocket. Short, but from her gut. Came out of nowhere.

> *Four days since you left me,*
> *Hundreds more to endure,*
> *Each one without the strength*
> *your love gives me.*

Zoë walks down the red-painted concrete stairwell, where she can hear the sneaker squeaks and yells from the gym. At the bottom of the stairs is the boys' locker room. She looks left, right, then opens the door. The smell overwhelms her. It is truly awful—sour and yeasty. For all the heartache she's been through, it makes her thankful she's a girl, and that most days, when she isn't on a mission to sneak a poem into her boyfriend's—her ex-boyfriend's—pants, she doesn't have to inhale something so noxious.

She eyes the aisle of lockers, unsure which is his. Should she open them all? She hesitates. It seems wrong, a violation of all these boys and their private belongings, their boxers and deodorants, things she has no right to see. But she can't think of another way, so she begins.

The first locker has a red backpack and argyle socks. Definitely not Henry's. The next, a pair of Old Navy corduroys. She hears the gym teacher, Mr. Tulosi, calling out to someone, a ball hitting the wall. Her heart beats fast, like she's some kind of criminal. Halfway through the lockers, she finds Henry's stuff. His black bag, Levi's with worn knees, and yellow T-shirt. She touches the T-shirt, feeling the cool softness of the fabric. Then she leans over and presses it to her face. His scent, oh, his scent, moves through her, filling the empty spaces. She loses herself in the shirt, letting her thoughts disappear, letting him reach her like this.

Until a door clangs open on the other side of the room, yanking her back.

Then it is all slow motion. Zoë flings the poem into Henry's locker. She runs toward the door through which she came. In her peripheral vision she sees the flash of one of the boys in Henry's gym class, coming into the room. He says, "Hey, what are you—?" But she's out of there, the door swinging behind her, and she heads for the stairs, nearly knocking over someone standing in her path.

"Oh. My. God."

Zoë's afraid to see whose arms she's run into, but she knows the voice.

"I've got her," Shannon says to Julia, who is coming down the stairs. Then to Zoë, "You've crossed over into psycho, haven't you?"

"What are you doing here?" Zoë asks. She tries to yank her arm away, but Shannon won't let go.

"What are *we* doing here?" Julia laughs.

"We're saving your life," Shannon says, not laughing at all. "And, I can see, not a moment too soon."

"I don't need saving," Zoë says, trying again to release her arm, but Shannon holds on firmly and guides her up the stairs.

"Girlfriend, you were in the boys' locker room."

"Just for a moment," Zoë says.

Julia laughs again. "Oh, well, then, that's okay." She takes Zoë's other arm. Zoë sees her PEACE and LOVE bracelets and feels oddly comforted. "You're one of those crazy girls. You're Erika Christensen in *Swimfan*."

"I am not!" Zoë tries yanking away from them again. "She wasn't his girlfriend in that movie. She seduced him for one night. Henry and I have six months of history."

Julia rolls her eyes. "Again with the six months."

Zoë's furious. Tears prick her eyes. "This is why I don't talk to you two. Those six months mattered to me. A lot. You don't even try to understand."

Shannon and Julia stop dragging her, and they stand in the hallway near the cafeteria. Shannon hugs her. Then Julia does. Zoë tries to stop her tears, the relentless tears that keep coming day after day.

"We want to understand," Shannon says. "We really do."

"I'm just trying to make you laugh," Julia says.

"I want him back," Zoë says, feeling herself crumple.

"Okay." Shannon holds her tightly. "We know you do. We want to help."

"No, you don't," Zoë says into Shannon's white angora sweater. "You want me to move on."

"True," Shannon says. "But we're beginning to understand that's not going to happen. So we'll proceed to Plan B."

"We will?" Julia asks, clearly not on board.

"Yes." Shannon releases Zoë and gives Julia a look. "It's either that or let her sink."

"Tell me about this Plan B, O guru," Julia says.

"Simple. We'll help Zoë get what she thinks she wants."

• • •

That evening the phone rings. Zoë, who is making a concerted effort to do her homework for the first time since D-Day, picks it up without thinking.

"Zoë."

Her heart leaps into her throat.

"Henry." She looks at the time: nine o'clock. Her skin tingles, actually tingles. She can't believe this is actually happening. For all her efforts, she didn't really believe he would come back to her. Not yet, not so easily. But here he is, calling her at their special time.

"I realized we had to talk."

"I'm so glad."

"You have to stop this."

She looks at the books on her desk, at her computer, the cursor blinking like some kind of warning.

"No more poems," Henry says. "No pictures. No hearts. Just stop."

A sick feeling spreads over her.

"You're being crazy," he goes on.

"I'm just trying to get you to see—"

"No." Henry cuts her off. "There's nothing to see. It's over."

"But it can't be," Zoë says, her voice low. She's trying so hard to maintain composure, to get out what she wants to say. "We were together for six months, Henry. Have you forgotten?"

"Of course not," he says, his voice soft, giving her hope.

"There's got to be some way of working things out," she says. She can hear the whine in her voice, the pleading. "Please. Let me back in."

"I'm sorry this sucks so bad for you, but you have to move on," Henry says. "It's over."

"No," Zoë says. She hears the way her voice rises. If she weren't so desperate, she would feel embarrassed. But that's a far-off place for her. Right now she's fighting to recapture her life.

"I have to go," Henry says.

Zoë's mind races, searching for a way to keep him on the phone. He's being awful, but at least he's engaging with her. At least he's not walking by her as if she doesn't exist, offering only a limp "Hi."

"I'll do anything," she says. Her voice is hoarse and pained like she has a sore throat. It's so ugly. All of this, ugly.

"Later, Zoë," Henry says.

Zoë grips the phone as she listens to it go dead. She waits, wondering how she'll make it to the next moment.

She moves, one aching muscle at a time, to get to her bed. She folds herself over, her arms around her knees, closing her body like a box. After a minute, or maybe an hour, or a lifetime for all she knows, she falls thankfully into a dark, dreamless sleep.

Day 7

Her first weekend without Henry. She lies in bed. She checks her e-mail. She does homework. She eats half an apple and throws the rest away.

Day 8

Just like the day before.

Day 9

A knock at her door. Zoë peeks out from beneath her pillow to see the clock: 7:30. She must have turned off her alarm without waking up, and now she's late. The knock comes again.

"Zoë, honey," she hears her mom say from the other side of the door. "Your bus will be here in twenty minutes."

"I'm not going to school."

Mom opens the door and sits on the bed. "Don't be like this."

Zoë rolls to her side and pulls the pillow over her head. Mom reaches to remove it.

"Will you just let me drop into despair in peace?"

"No," Mom says. "I most certainly won't. Get your butt up and out of this bed."

"I can't have one day to wallow?"

"No. You had the whole weekend."

"You know, just because you're always happy doesn't mean everyone else has to be."

"That's probably true," Mom says. "But you're my daughter, and sometimes I know you better than you know yourself. So I get to determine what's best for you."

"Fine," Zoë says, knowing she never wins when it comes to her mother.

She changes into jeans and throws a sweatshirt over the T-shirt she slept in. She brushes her teeth, but not her hair. She looks at herself in the mirror. Her eyes are dark. Her skin looks gray. Her brown hair, normally stick straight and tamed, is frizzed. A cowlick stands up on one side. It's her, but it's not anyone Zoë knows. It's a girl left bereft.

In the kitchen, Logan sits before a bowl overflowing with Cocoa Puffs. He doesn't look at her as she goes to the fridge and takes out the orange juice, just piles the mountain of little brown balls into his mouth. Zoë glimpses Mom in the dining room, still working on those curtains.

"Why do you let him eat that sugar?" Zoë asks.

"I can eat what I want." Logan still doesn't look at her.

Mom sighs. The sewing machine whirs and stops. "Honey, you went through a stage where you would only eat ham omelets. I had to make them for breakfast, lunch, and dinner if I wanted you to eat anything. You pick your battles with your kids. You'll see."

"No way." Zoë downs a glass of orange juice. "I'm never having kids." She sets the empty glass on the counter. She has no idea why she is saying any of this. She doesn't really care. She doesn't really care about anything anymore.

"Dad told me you made something for Henry," Mom says, changing the subject. "Are you sure that's such a good idea?"

Zoë frowns and places her glass in the dishwasher. "It doesn't matter." She doesn't say that as it turns out, it wasn't such a hot idea.

"I don't want you to get hurt," Mom says.

"Too late for that." Zoë pokes her head into the dining room, where red velvet covers the table. A finished curtain hangs over a window, hiding the view outside.

"You better go," Mom says. "It's seven-fifty."

Zoë looks back at Logan, who is now seeing how many Cocoa Puffs he can fit into his mouth at once. He grins at her and a couple of puffs pop out. She envies him the pleasure he gets from something so inane. These days eating is a chore, something Zoë does solely to survive.

She grabs her bag and heads outside, just in time to see her bus leaving. She watches it turn left onto Lincoln.

Perfect.

She considers asking Mom for a ride but thinks better of it and decides to walk. Maybe the fresh air will do her good. She straps her bag over her chest and starts walking, past the neighbors with their dandelion-filled lawn, past the other neighbors with their carefully designed garden of tulips and daffodils. She's seen the woman out there with weed killer, trying to ward off the dandelion seeds that float over from next door. Funny, Zoë thinks, how we live on the same earth, all of us with our different priorities and needs.

She thinks too, of course, of Henry.

He doesn't want to be with her, while she does with him. How did that happen? Six months ago she was the one who needed to be convinced. Henry had told Kylie, who'd told Julia that he liked her, and Julia had told Zoë. At first Zoë wasn't so sure they'd make a good couple. He was into music. She was into studying. He hung out with the stoners. She hung out with, well, with Shannon and Julia. He wasn't the kind of boy she would normally have gone for. Her type was Peter Ferguson, star basketball player, high scorer on the PSATs. Peter Ferguson, who had been her first kiss after a month of ninth-grade dating. It was nothing more than silly puppy love and the relationship ended amiably. No drama needed. Then, two years later, she met Henry. She remembers Henry approaching her for the first time at her locker after school. He asked her about the literary magazine she'd started, and they walked outside together, talking about stuff that she learned later Henry had little interest in. His interest was in her.

The next week was the beach trip, and their first kiss. Then came the next six months of her life, in which she slowly fell for him, and hard. And with that falling came the new things with which she filled her life: band practices; long hours at the Big Top, holding hands; time in Henry's bedroom, door open by his parents' rules, listening to him try out riffs on his guitar; and the times in his bedroom she misses the most, when they made out, for hours sometimes, until their lips were swollen and red.

She walks along Lincoln Avenue, remembering.

In the fall, when they were a relatively new couple, Henry bought them both sandwiches from the deli, and they took them to the playground for a picnic. They ate quickly beneath the park's huge spruce tree and then sat on the swings and pumped their legs to see who could go higher. She remembers feeling big, both because the swing that had once seemed so tall was now so low that she had to keep her legs lifted so as not to scrape the ground, and because she was here with Henry, this handsome boy who liked her enough to swing in a playground with her.

That same afternoon he invited her back to his house, where he showed her his two guitars, one Fender and one Gibson.

He described in great detail what made each special, the pick guards and pickups, truss rods and fret ends.

"Listen," he said, and he strummed the Gibson. "Do you hear that?" He set down the Gibson and strapped on the Fender. "Do you hear the difference?" She nodded, although she didn't. It was just the beginning of what she would come to know about guitars, more than she cared about, but information she treasured because it mattered to Henry.

Shannon and Julia were happy for her, but Zoë had less time for the things and people she cared about, including her best friends. Every love song Zoë hears confirms what it's like: you lose yourself in someone else. Eventually, you feel like you need him to breathe.

The cavern inside her chest yawns again. Will the pain ever lessen? Or will her heart always feel like a weighty stone?

Cars pass, filled with people moving through their lives. Ahead, a group of freshman girls laugh and chatter. Zoë wonders if life will ever feel effortless again.

• • •

Sam finds her in the hall.

"You look like hell," he says.

"Thanks." Zoë walks beside him, her head down. She fears she'll have another surprise sighting of Henry, which she learned the other day is equivalent to being socked in the gut.

"Is it about Henry?"

Zoë just looks at him. Is anything *not* about Henry?

"No luck, huh?"

"No." Zoë trudges on, wishing she could go back home and get into bed.

Sam is quiet beside her, letting her trudge in peace. Or so Zoë assumes.

"Have you given any thought to what we talked about?" he asks.

"I don't know what you mean," Zoë says. She smiles at a girl from calculus and realizes with an inward wince that she never got to the homework. Henry called and killed her before she ever got the chance.

"I mean going out with me."

Zoë grimaces. "Not now, Sam. I'm simply trying to live through the day."

Sam nods, disappointed. "Sorry it's been so rough."

"Me too."

"Well," he says as they split for separate classes, "I could make you feel better. A lot better, if you know what I mean."

Zoë rolls her eyes. "I'm sure."

He shrugs. "Can't blame a guy for trying."

• • •

Lunchtime again. The period invented to make those without lives feel exactly three inches tall. Zoë follows her friends outside. Another glorious day, full of grass smells and sunshine and piercing blue skies. She settles beside Shannon, who's telling them about her mother's fiftieth-birthday party, which she had to endure last weekend. Zoë looks down at the food she bought—an apple, macaroni and cheese, and a chocolate milk. Who was she kidding? She sets it next to her on the concrete ledge and looks up into the sunshine, trying to listen to Shannon.

And she sees him.

Henry, with another girl.

One of those girls she saw on the way to school. They're walking along the breezeway that leads to the outside entrance of the gym, smiling, talking, laughing. "Oh my god," Zoë says, interrupting Shannon. Zoë thinks she might throw up right there.

Julia and Shannon look at her and then follow her gaze.

"Breathe," Julia says. "They're just walking together."

"They're talking and laughing."

"But that's it," Shannon says. "Julia's right. You can't jump to conclusions."

"She's a freshman," Zoë says, watching them disappear behind the stairwell that leads to the gym.

"You don't know anything yet." Shannon puts her hand on Zoë's face and makes her look at her. "I know you. You've already got them in bed together."

"Oh my god." Zoë squeezes her eyes shut. She's in physical pain.

"Are we going to have to talk you down off this ledge?" Julia asks.

"Har har, Julia," Shannon says to her. Then to Zoë, "You have to get control of yourself. We're working on a plan, remember? Plan B."

Zoë shakes her head. "I have to talk to him."

"No." Shannon still holds her face firmly. "Julia, get her arms."

Zoë pulls away. "I don't need a straitjacket," she says. "I just need to talk with him."

"Zoë, talking to him is the worst idea in the world."

"Why?" There's that whine again. Since when has she become such a whiner?

"I hate to remind you, but he told you to leave him alone."

Zoë winces.

"We're going to come up with a way to help you, I promise," Shannon says. "But in the meantime, Zoë, read my lips: Don't. Act. Jealous."

Zoë frowns. That, she determines, is going to be impossible.

• • •

Zoë sits in the nurse's office, waiting for the nurse to take the thermometer from her mouth. She has never, ever faked illness before. Well, not since she was seven and went through a period of not wanting to be separated from her mother. But desperate times call for desperate measures. She can hear the nurse in the next room opening and closing drawers. Finally, after twenty years, she comes back in. She takes the thermometer, peers at it, and proclaims Zoë's temperature normal.

"I guess I'll go back to class," Zoë says. "I think I'm feeling better."

"You sure? Don't push yourself."

Zoë smiles, feeling bad now about lying. School nurses are always so gullible. She thanks the nurse, takes the hall pass—the thing she was after—and heads into the hallway. Two doors down is the activity room, where the yearbooks sit on shelves, including the yearbooks from the middle school around the corner. Many Lincoln High students went there, so it's a handy reference. Zoë searches the shelves, looking for last year's middle school yearbook. She spots it and carries it to the table. She glances at the door, aware that she has to move quickly. Anyone could come in. She flips to the face pages and scans them until she finds her: Madison Pella. Straight brown hair; big, pretty eyes; full lips. Zoë could not hate a person more. She goes to the sports pages, and there's Madison again. A cheerleader. *A cheerleader.* Henry used to laugh at the cheerleaders, saying how pathetic it was that they actually made a sport out of applauding and supporting another sport. He thought the whole thing was a waste of time.

"Why does it matter?" he said, laughing, being mean, when she suggested they go to the homecoming game. "Who cares if our town wins?"

"A lot of people care," Zoë said, feeling defensive.

"They're cattle," he said. "They should spend all

that energy trying to bring peace to the Middle East, or cleaning up oil spills."

"I don't see you doing any of those things," Zoë said.

"I make art," he countered. "I don't have to do those things."

Zoë had left it at that. She didn't like arguing with him, even though his argument seemed ridiculous.

Yet now here he is, talking and laughing—and who knows what else?—with one of those cattle. She wants to scream.

She closes the book and puts it back on the shelf. She checks to be sure the coast is clear, then heads back into the hallway. Maybe going to the nurse wasn't such a big lie. She feels utterly sick.

Day 10

In the morning, Zoë strides right past her bus stop. She walks purposefully down Lincoln Avenue. She has that feeling again, that little glimmer. It's not so much hope anymore, although she still holds on to the idea that she could get Henry back. The glimmer comes from having a reason to get up, a mission. It's a much better feeling than the alternative.

Near school, she sees them again. Freshman girls, chattering, cackling. Hate simmers beneath her skin. How easy for you, Zoë thinks. You've got what's rightfully mine. She breaks into a jog until she catches up.

"Madison," she says, a little winded.

Madison turns to look at her. She's as pretty up close and in person as she was in the yearbook. When she sees Zoë she smiles, an open, friendly smile. She's a whole head shorter than Zoë. Zoë imagines smacking her, the way they do in soap operas, sending her to the ground, some TV audience applauding her in the background.

"Hi?" Madison says.

"I'm Zoë." When Madison's expression doesn't change, Zoë adds, "Henry's girlfriend. Ex-girlfriend."

"Oh, right." Madison waves for her friends to go on without her.

"Has he mentioned me?" Zoë asks after waiting for Madison to say something more.

"Sure," Madison says. "I'm sorry things didn't work out."

I'll bet you are, Zoë thinks.

"Henry's cool."

Zoë stares at her. "He broke my heart. Crushed it into little tiny bits."

Madison frowns. She looks up ahead where her friends are, probably wishing she hadn't let them go. "I'm sorry, but why did you want to talk to me?"

Zoë smirks. How dare such a tiny freshman speak to her as though they are equals? "I saw you hanging out with him. I thought we should hang out too." She watches Madison closely for some reaction but there isn't any.

"Really?"

"Really." Zoë crosses her arms.

"What's the catch?"

Zoë laughs, trying to sound casual. "Why are you so paranoid?"

They look at each other, sizing each other up.

"Okay," Madison says, defiant. "When do you want to hang out?"

"Today after school. At the Big Top." Zoë is well aware that Henry might be there too.

"I'll see you there."

Zoë nods. As Madison turns to catch up with her friends, Zoë thinks of something.

"He doesn't want a girlfriend, you know," she calls after Madison.

Madison stops and spins around. "Who said I wanted to be his girlfriend?"

"And he thinks cheerleading is stupid."

Madison narrows her eyes. "I'm also a singer," she says, and with that heart-stopping information, she runs toward her friends. Zoë twists her mouth and looks after her. A singer is not good. A singer is someone Henry would like. A swirling feeling starts in her belly.

• • •

That afternoon, Zoë sits in the Big Top with Madison. She smiles.

"That's a really cute shirt."

"Thanks." Madison smiles back, but looks doubtful.

"So." Zoë maintains her smile, trying to think of something to say. "You're a singer?"

"I sing with the choral group. I'm the head soloist."

"I guess that means you're really good." Zoë tries not to seem concerned.

Madison laughs a carefree laugh, a laugh that shows she's never had her heart trampled on. "That's what the teacher says, but I don't know."

Zoë hates her from the bottom of her soul. "Sing a few bars," she says.

"No." Madison smiles that cute, annoying smile again. "Not here."

"Come on. No one will hear."

"Really?"

Zoë internally rolls her eyes. She can't believe how easy this girl is. "Go ahead."

Madison licks her lips, takes a breath, and sings the opening lines of "Somewhere Over the Rainbow." She really is very good.

Zoë holds her composure. "Has Henry heard you sing?"

Something flashes over Madison's face at the mention of Henry's name and Zoë knows for sure she likes him.

"Not that I'm aware of," Madison says.

What is that supposed to mean? Zoë wonders. Does Madison think Henry might have heard her singing in the hallways and followed the sound like some siren song?

"I write poetry," Zoë blurts. "And I dance."

"Wow." Madison feigns fascination. "Are you any good?"

"Yes," Zoë says. "As a matter of fact I am."

They sit a moment longer, staring each other down, and then they stand.

"Zoë?" Zoë turns to see Shannon. "What are you doing here?"

Zoë smiles, but there's no putting one over on Shannon.

"Do you know Madison?" Zoë holds her smile.

"I'm Shannon." Shannon holds her hand out to Madison, who takes it limply with her fingers, then lets go.

"Real nice to meet you." Madison's smile is fake too.

"Hey," Shannon says, looking at Zoë, "can I speak with you a moment?"

Zoë shrugs. She knows what's coming. "I guess that would be okay."

"This was really fun," Madison says, reaching behind her chair for her jacket. "I have to go anyway."

"Right," Zoë says. "Let's do it again soon."

Once Madison is gone, Shannon shakes her head.

"So now you're befriending the new girlfriend."

"She is not Henry's new girlfriend!"

Shannon waits.

"I can make a new friend if I want. There are people in the world besides you and Julia."

Shannon sits in the seat Madison abandoned and waits for Zoë to sit too.

"Okay, fine. My motives weren't exactly angelic."

Shannon nods. "You want information."

"Maybe."

"And what do you intend to do with this information?"

Zoë shrugs. "I haven't thought it through yet." She can hear the defensiveness in her voice.

"That's the problem," Shannon says. "You're impulsive. Don't you see the trouble you keep getting yourself into?"

"You don't understand," Zoë says.

"So you keep saying."

"I can't just do nothing."

"Why not? Why can't you wait for Julia and me to help you? We want to help you, Zoë." Shannon starts tapping her foot. She also twirls a dark curl, which is what she does whenever she's frustrated.

"Because," Zoë says, frustrated too. She wishes she didn't have to explain. She wishes her friends just knew what she needed right now. Her voice goes soft, raw with emotion. "It hurts too much."

Shannon takes Zoë's hand, but Zoë can tell she doesn't really get it.

Day 11

Zoë traps Niles in the hallway.

"I have to get to class," he says.

She smiles, thinking of how he thought she was a Yoko. How he may well have been the springboard to Henry's decision to break up with her. A tiny growl rises into her throat.

"I just have a quick question," she says. "You won't be late. What's going on between Madison and Henry?"

Niles guffaws and shakes his head. "No way. I'm not getting involved."

"So there is something." He starts to walk, but Zoë pushes him back.

"This isn't my business, Zoë."

"I'm making it your business."

He laughs again. "Since when did you become so hard?" he asks.

She watches him, trying to read how he meant that. As far as she can tell, he's being perfectly honest. Is she really hard? Is that what she's become?

"I don't know," she says. "I guess since your friend crushed the soft right out of me."

Niles shakes his head. "I didn't know you had this bitchy side."

Zoë isn't trying to be bitchy. She's just telling the truth. "So, you're not going to tell me anything about Madison."

Niles raises his hands in the air. "I know nothing," he says.

She doesn't believe him. But she moves aside anyway and lets him go.

Day 12

Zoë traps David Jefferson.

"What do you know?"

"What do I know about what?" he asks. He looks a little scared, which is good, Zoë decides. She can work with scared.

"Henry and that girl Madison."

David backs away. "You're crazy, know that? Nuts." He twirls a finger at his ear to emphasize his point.

Day 13

It's Friday night. The only thing worse than an upcoming weekend for a girl who's just been dumped is the knowledge that the ex might be out there celebrating his weekend with someone else. Zoë's parents rent *Super Size Me,* a documentary about fast food, and the whole family gathers in the den to watch. Zoë knows why her parents got this movie. Considering the things they allow Logan to eat, they obviously aren't overly concerned about the state of food consumption in the culture. They want to get Zoë's mind off the breakup, off happy endings and romance. She appreciates the effort, even though it doesn't work. Logan reenacts the throw-up scene again and again, thinking it's the funniest thing he's ever seen. Zoë tolerates him for a few minutes, then goes straight to bed, eager for unconsciousness.

Day 14

Shannon invites Zoë and Julia over to hang out, but Mom and Dad suggest the possibility of Zoë's babysitting Logan while they go out for dinner. This sounds better to Zoë. She loves her friends, but the world out there is too dangerous right now. Better to stay home where she can control what comes at her, where she isn't faced with one Henry land mine after another.

She and Logan eat macaroni and cheese, then say good-bye to Mom and Dad.

"Don't let Logan overdo it with the sugar," Mom says, gathering her purse and jacket.

"And no R-rated movies," Dad adds.

"Don't worry," Zoë tells them. She stands near the door. "I won't let him do anything."

Mom kisses her. Zoë smells her perfume, which her mother only wears when she and Dad go out alone. After all these years, Mom still seems giddy to be on a date with her husband. It's not right, Zoë thinks. They're middle-aged. In a fair world, *she* would be the one having fun on a Saturday night.

"Don't think I'm going to listen to anything you say," Logan says as soon as the door closes. He goes to the kitchen and opens the freezer. He takes out an ice cream bar, then sits on the couch with the remote.

"Dad said no R-rated movies."

Logan raises his arm to flip her the bird. Some movie flashes onto the TV screen, one of those high-testosterone flicks where something explodes every five minutes. Zoë sighs and goes upstairs. The truth is, she doesn't really care what Logan does. She closes her bedroom door and turns on the radio. Some love song, whining and angst-ridden, blares from the speakers. She never noticed before D-Day that pretty much every song she hears is about losing and longing for love. On one hand, it makes her feel better that she's not all alone. On the other, it makes her want to hide under her bed. Is this what love is all about? Deprivation and pain? Is this what's in store for her for the remainder of her life?

She opens her closet and takes down the journal she kept during her and Henry's relationship. She walks it over to her desk and inhales deeply. She does not want to take a heart-wrenching stroll down memory lane. No way. Rather, she's looking for clues. The possibility has entered her mind that Henry was interested in Madison while they were still together, that this is the real reason he pink-slipped her. Zoë can imagine Shannon tsk-tsking her for spending time on something so ineffectual. But she flips through the pages, unwilling to look at her happiness from when they were together—the pain is too palpable—and finds the last few entries.

March 1

I love H. I love everything about him—his shaggy brown hair, his soft long-sleeve shirts, the way he walks, the way he says my name. Shannon called and we watched Gossip Girl *together over the phone. I didn't say anything to her because she thinks I'm stupid when I do stuff like this, but doesn't Nate look just a little like H? He even acts like him, all quiet and brooding. Sigh.*

March 5

Tonight was open mike at the Big Top. I hope it's safe to write here that sometimes I wish H spent more time thinking about me than his damn guitar. Oops. Did I really just write that?

Nothing interesting there, so Zoë flips forward. She stops at this entry.

March 11
H and I hung out at the Big Top after band practice today. He's excited about their new sound and couldn't wait to get home to write some songs. He's been online the past hour or so but hasn't answered my IMs. Trying not to freak. Just do my homework like a good girl.

Zoë puts a hand to her mouth. How could she have been so stupid? She opens her laptop and signs into her e-mail. There's a new message from Shannon with the subject line "Plan B," but she ignores it and goes to the deleted files to look for March 11. All she finds are a couple of e-mails from Julia. She stands and paces. That whole time she thought Henry was happy, focusing more on his music than her. It wasn't his music. It was Madison. That whole time! Her eyes dart around the room. She has to find a way to know for sure. Numb, she throws on a jacket and slides her feet into her pink fuzzy slippers. She marches downstairs.

"Don't do anything dumb," she tells Logan. He looks at her, confused, as she goes out the door into the night. A small part of her mind hears her own voice echo back to her: *Don't do anything dumb,* but she's too incensed to listen. She starts to hear other things: the scuff of her slippers on the concrete sidewalk, the quickening of her breath as she picks up her pace. It all seems straightforward and uncomplicated. She must find out what Henry was doing online March 11, and the only way to do that is to go to the source.

She walks for twenty minutes, following the familiar route until she reaches his house. It glows with yellow light in the darkness. She can see the TV on in the family room. Henry's room is dark, as she expected. Tonight is open-mike night. Another thought comes to her that makes her wince: Maybe he's with Madison. She looks down the long walkway to the Boles' front door. She has no plan, she realizes. The maple tree is still there, of course, but that's out of the question. Henry's windows are closed. She has no choice but to walk up to the front door and face her demons head-on.

She presses the doorbell and waits, her heart thudding in her chest.

Mrs. Bole answers. Her open face drops into worry when she sees Zoë standing there.

"Zoë?" Mrs. Bole peers at her, perplexed. Her eyes travel down to Zoë's fuzzy slippers.

"I'm sure you're wondering what I'm doing here," Zoë starts. "I mean, it's been a couple weeks now since Henry and I broke up. And then there was that incident in your yard." She laughs, trying to lighten the mood, but Mrs. Bole's expression doesn't change. "Well, I took your advice. I went home and I've moved on. I'm all better now!" Zoë is aware that her voice is too high, so she smiles again, trying to gather herself.

"Zoë," Mrs. Bole says. "What *are* you doing here?"

"It makes sense that you're concerned," Zoë says. "You probably think I'm out of my mind." She smiles, but once again Mrs. Bole doesn't join her. "I'll get right to it. I'm here because I left something that's very important to me, and I need it back."

Mrs. Bole looks doubtful.

"Henry didn't realize I left it here, or else I'm sure he would have returned it."

Mrs. Bole cocks her head now. "Can I ask what it is? Perhaps I can retrieve it for you."

Zoë's mind races as she tries to come up with what that thing might be, and, more importantly, why she has to retrieve it herself. "Henry didn't tell you about my fungus?" she blurts.

Mrs. Bole's face bunches. She puts a hand to her neck. "Fungus?"

Zoë cringes. What has she gotten herself into? "I see he never told you. Yes, I have a fungus. It isn't the worst fungus in the world, but with all the stress of these past few weeks it's flared up again. Badly. And the cream I treat it with, which I have to apply directly to the fungus, you understand, that cream is here in Henry's room."

Mrs. Bole steps aside from the doorway, a look of revulsion on her face. "Please come in and get it," she says in a scratchy voice.

"Thanks." Zoë smiles pleasantly again and races up the stairs to Henry's room.

When she gets there, she quickly realizes she may

have made a mistake. A big one. Before her is everything in the world that is Henry—his worn jeans in a heap on the floor, clean clothes folded on top of his dresser, textbooks and papers on his desk, a chewed pen, the ceramic bowl he made in kindergarten where he now keeps his picks, the wrinkled sheets on his unmade bed, a dip in the pillow from when he last lay there. His two guitar stands, the Gibson not there. Pain rips through her body with little fireworks explosions. Walking in here, she has stepped on every land mine there is.

But there's no time for that. Mrs. Bole won't leave her alone for long. Zoë forces herself toward Henry's computer, to touch the shirt that is slung over the seat of the chair and drop it to the floor, and to sit. She wakes his computer from sleep mode and logs on to his e-mail account. She works quickly, her mind and body steeled against the sensory experience that surrounds her, the smells and sights of the boy she still loves but can't have. She finds his archived e-mails and scans the dates until she finds March 11. Her muscles are tight, already guarded, prepared. But she finds nothing. All the e-mails are from Niles, David Jefferson, and, of course, her. She opens one of the ones to Niles. It reads:

Dude, I finally found the Stratocaster you're looking for after much research. You owe me. Check it out. H.

There's a link to the guitar.

Oh.

He was researching guitars. That's why he didn't answer her IMs that night.

Zoë hears the clicking of Mrs. Bole's heels, so she logs out. She places the shirt back on the chair. And in the seconds before Mrs. Bole appears at the doorway, she lifts the chewed pen and stuffs it into her jacket pocket.

"Find what you're looking for?" Mrs. Bole asks as she comes in.

"I did." Zoë presses her fist against the inside of her pocket to make a bulge. "Got it right here."

"Okay, then." Mrs. Bole glances down at the pocket and up again. She gestures for Zoë to follow her out of the room.

At the front door, Mrs. Bole frowns. "Take care of that fungus," she tells Zoë.

"I will." Zoë nods and starts down the walkway. She turns once to see Mrs. Bole quickly close the door.

Researching guitars. Zoë tells herself this is good news. Henry probably wasn't interested in another girl while he was seeing her. But even with this news, she feels just as empty, just as broken as before. In fact, having been in Henry's room and seeing all his things, she's reminded that his life has been moving forward without her. She reaches into her pocket and takes out the chewed pen. In the light from the streetlamps she can see his tooth marks. She runs her finger over them, feeling the little bumps and ridges like Braille. The bottom line is she can't be sure whether or not he was interested in someone else. She can't be sure whether he broke up with her because he wants to focus on his band or whether he doesn't love her anymore. No evidence will ever give her the answers she wants.

The moon is a thin sliver. The dark trees loom above her, lining the street. Without thinking, she doesn't turn off First Street. She continues on, her heart heavy, until she reaches the Big Top. Through the window, she sees Henry on the far side of the café near the stage. He sits with the rest of the band, watching some girl strumming a guitar onstage. Zoë's cavern yawns. So many girls out there he can love, so many girls who are not her. She hasn't thought much about it until now. It's been too painful to go there. But he will. He'll love another, if not here in Portland, then in college. He'll keep moving forward, away from her. Eventually, she'll be a girlfriend he had in high school, a tiny nothing in the large expanse of what his life will become.

She opens the door and walks toward him, vaguely aware of her fuzzy pink slippers. It doesn't matter anymore, does it? At this point she can only hope for tiny drops of relief here and there, a drizzle in a vast, dry desert. He can give her that, can't he? With all he's taken, can't he give her this one thing?

As she approaches his table, he looks up and registers her presence. He looks surprised and then irritated.

"Zoë, what are you doing?"

The other guys get up from the table, giving them space. She sees Niles smirk.

"I need you to tell me the truth," she says once

they're alone. The girl onstage strums on, playing some folky tune.

"What the hell, Zoë?" Henry rubs his head, making his flyaway hair even more so. He looks over at his bandmates, who are standing near the barista's counter. He's clearly embarrassed. "What are you talking about?"

"I need to know why you broke up with me."

"I told you why."

"I'm thinking you didn't tell me everything."

"You're thinking wrong."

"What about Madison?"

"Madison?"

"The cheerleader, Henry. I thought you hated cheerleaders."

Henry laughs. It's not a nice laugh. It's a laugh that means he's maintaining his composure when what he'd really like is to get up and walk away. "I hardly know that girl, Zoë."

Zoë scowls. She doesn't believe him.

"I'm about to perform." He gestures to the guys. "Do you mind?"

Zoë looks down. Her fuzzy slippers are coated with grime from the walk. She must look like such a fool. "You stopped loving me," she says softly. Of course the tears come, hot and sharp.

Henry sighs. "Oh, man," he says. He leans his head back, his hands on his forehead like she's putting him through something unpleasant. Like *she's* putting *him* through something!

The girl stops strumming her guitar. She says into the microphone, "Thanks for coming out tonight, folks."

"Look," Henry says. "You've got to move on, okay? You've got to get over it."

Zoë knows he's right. It's what everyone's telling her. But she's finding that it's not so easy to just turn off feelings. Doesn't it count for anything that she still loves him? "I'm trying," she tells him.

He stands and puts his hand to the small of her back and walks her to the door. She walks along beside him, like a dog on a leash. Anything to feel his hand on her again.

"Nice seeing you, though." He smiles his polite smile.

Zoë considers her options: she can run out the door screaming and crying, she can grab a butter knife from one of the tables and commit hara-kiri, or she can simply walk away. Even though it's the only option that doesn't mirror her insides, she decides on the last one.

"Later," Henry says as he opens the door and waits for her to exit. Zoë feels she's been dismissed.

She starts her walk home. Whoever invented the word *heartsick* had it exactly right. Her heart feels physically ill. She wishes she really could yank it out of her chest. She should have grabbed that butter knife while she could. She's reached her end. No more trying to get through this alone. No more ignoring everyone else. She needs help, or she's not sure she'll survive.

When she opens the door of her house, her parents descend upon her.

"Where were you, young lady?" Mom shrieks.

"What in God's name were you thinking?" Dad says. "We trusted you to watch your brother. And you disappeared."

Zoë gasps. She had honestly forgotten. "I'm sorry," she says.

"I could have been murdered," Logan says. She looks up to see him sitting at the top of the stairs. He's in Stormtrooper pajamas.

"That's enough out of you," Dad says to him. "Get back in bed." And then to Zoë, "Sorry doesn't cut it. You're grounded."

Zoë nods. "Okay."

"For a week," Mom says.

"Only a week?" Logan whines from the stairs.

"What did I just say to you?" Dad yells. Logan slinks back to his bedroom.

"We're disappointed," Mom says to Zoë. She notices Zoë's dirty pink slippers, and her expression changes from anger to concern. "What's going on with you?"

"I don't know," Zoë answers, which is the honest truth.

"Well, you'll have plenty of time to think about it," Dad says.

Zoë nods and hauls her body up the stairs. She doesn't care about being grounded. If she were still with Henry, she'd be devastated. But nothing really matters anymore. In her room, she opens her laptop and clicks on Shannon's e-mail.

Julia and I would like to talk over some ideas for Plan B. Remember, we want to help you, Z. Are you alive? Call me. Shan

Zoë writes back.

Just barely.

Day 15

Zoë turns up her music as loud as it will go, but it doesn't drown out the way she feels—miserable.

Day 16

Zoë turns over the calculus test on her desk. They have thirty minutes to complete it. She stares at the numbers and symbols, few of them familiar. When did she lose face in math? Calculus used to be one of her strongest classes. Most classes were her strongest classes. She squeezes her eyes shut, wondering what's happened to her.

Afterward, Shannon and Julia ambush her in the hallway. It's lunchtime.

"You're coming over after school," Shannon says.

She loops her arm through Zoë's and begins to walk. "No excuses."

"Can't," Zoë says apologetically. "I'm grounded."

"Grounded?" Julia asks. "I thought you babysat this weekend. What could you possibly have done wrong?"

"You don't want to know."

Shannon and Julia stare at her.

"Oh, yes, we do," Shannon says.

"Let's just say I didn't actually babysit."

"Because instead you were . . ." They aren't going to let this go.

Zoë cringes. "Breaking into Henry's e-mail account," she whispers.

Julia laughs.

"Oh, Z." Shannon frowns.

"You can say it," Zoë says as they enter the cafeteria. "I've lost my mind. Gone off the deep end. Send in the men in white coats."

Shannon shakes her head. "You're not doing well. I'll give you that."

"I don't understand," Julia says. She picks up a red tray and slides it onto the metal-slatted counter. "Why didn't you call us if you were starting to freak?"

"I honestly don't know." Zoë looks at the greasy orange disks they call chicken patties and shakes her head at the cafeteria lady. "I think there might be something short-circuiting in my brain."

"It's called a broken heart," Shannon says.

"Like you know anything about it." Julia snorts. She plucks a red Jell-O from a cart.

"That has poison in it," Shannon says.

"Does not."

"Red Dye Number Five."

Julia takes a bite off the top, then puts her hand to her throat as if she's struggling to breathe. "I think I'll live."

"Anyway," Shannon says, "you don't have to have experienced heartache to know it can make you crazy. I read once about this woman in New York who didn't have any money to get to her lover, so she tried swimming across the Hudson River and died of hypothermia."

Julia and Zoë laugh.

"Why didn't she just walk across the bridge?" Zoë says, still laughing.

"She wasn't near a bridge."

Zoë and Julia give each other a look.

"What?" Shannon says, defensive. "It could happen."

They pay the cashier and, for a change, stay inside and sit at a table.

"At least I'm not swimming across the Willamette," Zoë says.

"Yet." Julia smiles at her. Zoë smiles back. It's such a relief to be with her friends again. What was she thinking, trying to get through this ordeal on her own?

Niles walks by, wearing headphones over his thick black hair. He smiles at Zoë. "No fuzzy slippers today?" he says as he passes.

"Ha ha," Zoë says to him. Her friends raise their eyebrows.

"Was that a flirt?" Shannon asks.

"Methinks that was a flirt," Julia says.

"No." Zoë looks back at Niles. He tosses a crumpled bag into the trash and pushes open the doors to the hallway. They slowly close behind him. At least she doesn't think so.

"That's it," Shannon says with a smile. "Plan B: We get a new guy involved to make Henry jealous."

"And to do that," Julia says to Zoë, "you need to look hot."

"Because I don't look hot now?" Zoë is being sarcastic. She hasn't washed her hair in three days and she's pretty sure she's wearing two different-colored socks. She pulls up her jeans so her friends can see.

"Niles can be our target," Shannon tells Julia.

"No," Zoë says. "He's Henry's best friend."

"Exactly. Guys are like dogs," Shannon continues. "If you stoke Niles's interest, Henry might act fast to maintain his alpha status."

"I don't follow." Zoë's curious now.

"If a guy thinks some other guy likes his girl, he gets possessive."

"In other words," Julia says, "Henry pissed on you. He doesn't want to smell his best friend's piss on you too."

"You're grossing me out," Zoë says, pushing her tray away.

"But are you feeling us?"

"I guess so." She cocks her head, not sure yet. She loves Henry, not Niles. She doesn't know how to pretend to love someone.

"But first you have to look hot. If for nothing else, so you can feel better about yourself," Shannon says.

"And so we can feel better about you too," Julia adds with a sneer.

• • •

Zoë ducks as she passes the activity room. She knows this is childish behavior, but maturity hasn't exactly been her forte these past couple of weeks. Sam is in there, along with the others who work on the literary magazine. The magazine was her invention, born of her wanting to share her own work. Ms. Carter and the principal helped her get the project off the ground. Sam came to work on it right away. At first Zoë assumed it was because of his crush on her, but over time she realized he actually cared about the magazine. She has to admit they had fun together, looking at artwork and poetry and consulting on decisions. But she hasn't been to the meetings in close to five months. The whole thing has been rolling along without her. Part of her is relieved, but another part feels forlorn. This was *her* idea, and now she doesn't even know what they named it.

"What are you doing?" Sam asks as he pops out of the room and spots Zoë.

"Oh," she says, standing up straight and thinking quickly. "I lost my contact lens."

"You don't wear glasses."

Zoë gives him a firm look. "You don't know everything about me, Sam."

Sam stares back, a smirk hidden under a calm facade. "We're having a lit magazine meeting," he says.

"Yeah. I can't come, though. I'm grounded. I'm supposed to go straight home."

Sam shrugs. "I thought you *wanted* to do the lit magazine. It was your baby."

Zoë puts her hands on her hips, defensive. "I got busy. I have a life, Sam. You should try it sometime."

A wounded look moves across his face, and instantly Zoë regrets her words. "You've changed," Sam says; then he opens the door to the activity room and disappears inside.

Zoë hesitates, wondering whether she should follow him and apologize. Whether she should also join the meeting. Being grounded doesn't really count. She's allowed to participate in school activities. She peeks in and sees Sam talking with a girl, Anna something. Zoë can't remember her last name. The rest sit huddled in a group, deep in discussion. Zoë is so out of the loop, she can't even imagine what the hot topic could be. She walks off, a sickened feeling wiring its way through her body. Maybe Sam does know everything about her. She has changed, and she has no idea who she's become.

· · ·

In Zoë's room that afternoon, Shannon and Julia pull clothes out of her closet and throw them on Zoë, who's sitting on the bed.

"How did you ever land a guy with these clothes?" Julia asks. She's wearing a tight black shirt and denim skirt. Her motorcycle boots just graze the bottoms of her knees. Julia may not be interested in love, but Zoë has to admit that Julia knows how to put an outfit together.

"Very funny." Zoë holds up a green sweater they threw at her.

"I'm not being funny," Julia says. "Your clothes suck. Maybe . . ."

Shannon glances at Julia. "What are you thinking?"

"I'm thinking I'll run home and bring stuff from my wardrobe."

While Julia's gone, Shannon sits next to Zoë.

"It's been tough, huh?" she asks.

"Unbelievably tough."

Right then Mom pokes her head through Zoë's open door.

"Everything okay in here? Can I get you girls something?"

Zoë shakes her head. Mom said her friends could come over just until Dad gets home, which won't be until late. Mom knows Zoë's grounded, but she feels bad. She knows Zoë has had a hard time lately.

101

"Thank you, Mrs. Gill." Shannon smiles sweetly. Parents always love Shannon. She's the kind of friend about whom they say "Why can't you be more like Shannon?"

After Mom is gone, Zoë says, "I loved him."

"I know." Shannon puts her hand on Zoë's arm.

"I still love him."

Shannon just listens.

"But the worst part is I don't know who I am without him."

Shannon nods, encouraging her to go on.

"Do you think I changed with Henry?"

Shannon bites her lip, clearly uncertain what she should say. "Yeah, Z. I do."

"I can't even remember who I was before him."

"I do."

"Really?"

"You were interested in writing and doing well in school. You put that crazy, obsessive energy of yours into creating stuff."

Zoë stares at the clothes crumpled on her bed and considers this. "That person feels a zillion miles away."

Shannon ties her curly hair into a knot on top of her head. Zoë has always envied Shannon her hair. And these days she's utterly sick of feeling like other people have what she doesn't.

"I still see that spark in you," Shannon says.

Zoë looks down at her bed, where she's wringing a shirt in her hands. "You guys stayed friends with me through all of it."

Shannon smiles. "Of course we did."

"I really appreciate that."

"That's nice, Z, but you're our friend. We love you. We see you through things. You see us through things. That's the way it works."

Julia returns then, panting. She lives nearby, but she really must have run. In her arms is a big pile of clothes. "No boy will be able to survive these," she says as she dumps them on Zoë's bed.

"You guys are the best," Zoë says. Tears pop into her eyes, for the millionth and a half time in the past few weeks. But these tears aren't from sadness. These tears are from feeling thankful, blessed even, for the first time since D-Day.

Day 17

Zoë does inventory: Tall black boots, check. Short skirt, check. Lacy top, check. Push-up bra, check. She glances up the stairwell and considers the number of steps she has to climb to get to her locker. She loves her friends. She wouldn't trade them for anything. But maybe Plan B wasn't the best idea. She begins her ascent, aware with each step that her skirt slides up a little too high. She prays no boys are behind her, getting a view. A couple of girls she knows from class say hi but glance at her oddly, surely because her hair looks like someone attacked it with a curling iron, or because of the fifteen pounds of makeup Julia and Shannon suggested she wear. There's a reason Logan laughed his head off at her this morning when she came through the kitchen as inconspicuously as she could. At least she got away before her mother could see her.

She grips her bag. Why, why, why did she listen to Shannon and Julia?

At the top of the three flights, Zoë makes her way to her locker. The boots make her stumble. She's aware that her bra, which she hardly fills, has shifted, possibly to the side of her torso. She strides forward anyway. Just like in all the teen movies, every single person stops what he or she is doing to watch her go by. She keeps her gaze straight, unwilling to register the expressions on the faces around her. She opens her locker and, using the door as a shield, sticks her hand down her shirt to straighten the bra.

Niles peeks around the side. "Hey there."

"Oh!" Zoë nearly jumps out of her skin. Slowly she removes her hand from down her shirt. She looks into her locker, wondering about the possibility of climbing in and shutting herself inside.

Niles's eyes travel from the top of her head down to her boots. "Wow! What happened?"

"What do you mean?" Zoë smiles, attempting innocence. But she is nervous. Does she look as ridiculous as she feels?

"Considering you were in fuzzy slippers not long ago, I think it's a valid question."

Zoë shrugs, pretending she's not wishing she could spontaneously combust. "I felt like dressing up today."

"Interesting choice," Niles says, and walks away.

Zoë blinks. What is *that* supposed to mean? she wonders. She honestly thinks she might hate Niles. Shannon and Julia want her to flirt with him, reel him in, but every instinct in her body tells her to run fast the other way.

She closes the locker door and sees Henry. *Wham!* It's like a grenade slamming into her chest. It takes a good five seconds for her to find her breath again. He's walking down the hall toward his class, that familiar lope. He's alone, books tucked under his arm. Her heart does a looping dance of sorrow and joy.

He sees her, and she watches as his eyes widen.

"Hi," she says as casually as she can, just like she practiced for an hour before coming to school today.

This time he doesn't say hi back. He doesn't walk by her as though she's no one. No. His mouth drops open. His face goes red. This time, she's the one who looks away first. She puts a hand over her mouth to hide her grin. *Oh my god,* she thinks. It worked. It really worked. After these weeks of writing poems, climbing trees, and breaking into e-mail, of crying and emptiness, it turns out all she needed to do was put on a short skirt. She shakes her head in disbelief. Another feeling creeps up too, one she doesn't expect. Disappointment. She can't believe that looking "hot" is the thing that stirs Henry, not the poems, not her declarations of love.

She's the one who gets to walk away this time. It feels good, so different from before. Maybe Shannon and Julia were right. All she needed was to reclaim her self-confidence—and all it took was a little makeup and cleavage. She starts to move, shimmying her hips—until one boot catches the other and down she goes. She lands on her belly and slides a few feet. Her books go flying out in front of her. Her purse skitters across the hallway. She stays still a moment, assessing the situation. Her elbows hurt. So do her knees. Her skirt, she is pretty sure, is flipped up, exposing the cotton granny underpants she put on this morning without thought. She reaches around to check and finds that her assessment is accurate. She folds down the skirt, stands, and brushes herself off. She bends to get her books, ignoring her Lincoln High spectators except for the one who hands her the purse. This one she quietly thanks. She doesn't dare turn to see whether Henry is still standing there. It's enough to assume he is. She raises her head high and keeps walking.

"Have a nice trip?" Sam asks as he comes up beside her.

"How original." Zoë reaches around her books to feel her elbows, which are pretty badly chafed.

"What's up with the outfit?"

Zoë shrugs. She doesn't want to have to explain to Sam. They walk toward class. "Can't a girl clean up a little?"

"It's not you."

Zoë sighs. She can still feel everyone's eyes on her. A couple of boys whoop. She cringes, knowing that at least a few kids saw her underpants. Sam is right. Why does Sam always have to be right? "It can become me," she tries.

Sam grimaces. "I don't understand you lately."

He leaves her at her classroom, and she watches him walk off. She doesn't understand herself lately either.

• • •

That afternoon, Zoë goes into the bathroom to adjust her bra and finds Madison applying lip gloss at the mirror. Zoë is so not in the mood, but she gives Madison her best fake smile anyway. Madison eyes her up and down.

"You look really good," Madison says unhappily.

Zoë shrugs. "This old thing?" All she needs is for Madison to catch on to her plan. She goes into a stall and starts working on her bra.

"Did Henry see you?" Madison asks.

Zoë frowns. Why would Madison ask about Henry unless she liked him? "I'm not sure," Zoë says.

"I'll bet he'd think you look good too."

"Maybe."

"I heard you wiped out."

Zoë unlatches the door, annoyed. "Where did you hear that?"

"Are you kidding?" Madison says. She snaps her purse closed and heads for the door. "This is Lincoln High."

Zoë doesn't say that Madison, lowly freshman that she is, doesn't know the first thing about Lincoln High. Instead she says, "Nice bumping into you."

"Yeah," Madison says as she walks out. "Let's do it again soon."

• • •

Julia whistles when Zoë walks into English lit and takes a seat.

"Shut up," Zoë mouths.

A note lands on her desk.

Did Niles see you?

Zoë scribbles *yes* and sends it back.

Henry?

Zoë turns and nods. Julia writes another note and sends it over. It skids off Zoë's desk and lands by her tall-booted, beginning-to-blister foot.

I heard you took a serious spill.

Zoë presses her lips together. God, she hates this school.

After class, Ms. Carter asks her to stay a moment, so Zoë hobbles to the front.

"What's going on, Zoë?" the teacher asks.

Zoë looks down, embarrassed. "It was Julia's idea," she says. "I look stupid, I know."

Ms. Carter furrows her brows, confused. "With your class performance."

"Oh." Zoë winces. She doesn't know how much more humiliation she can take today.

"You're one of my best students. But lately you've been slipping." Ms. Carter taps a pencil on a book. *Pride and Prejudice*. Zoë hasn't read the assigned chapters yet. Case in point, she supposes. The rest of her classmates empty out of the classroom.

"I know. I'm sorry."

"Is this about the boyfriend?"

"Sort of."

"Listen, Zoë," Ms. Carter says. She leans against the desk, her hips spreading beneath her wool skirt. "I'm going to tell you something important."

Zoë nods. Here it comes: one of Ms. Carter's infamous monologues. It's been too many days of getting advice she doesn't want to hear. She braces herself for more.

"No guy is worth ruining your life over—even though in all the classics, a happy ending almost always involves marriage or true love." She gestures toward the Jane Austen book on her desk. "I'm afraid there aren't many stories for girls where happiness is found without a man. But there are some. Keep reading and you'll find them."

Zoë watches Ms. Carter, thinking about actually taking this in.

"Don't let a boy determine your happiness."

"That's what my friends say," Zoë tells her.

"Your friends are smart women."

"But they've never been in love," Zoë says.

Ms. Carter smiles. "Love is overrated, Zoë. Books."

She holds up *Pride and Prejudice*. "Books are where it's at."

Zoë grimaces. Ms. Carter can be such a dork. Still, Zoë knows she should probably listen to what she has to say. Chances are her ideas are better than Zoë's friends'.

"Thanks, Ms. Carter."

"Do the reading," Ms. Carter calls as Zoë limps out the door.

• • •

As she's leaving school, Zoë stops again outside the activity room. The literary magazine group isn't meeting today, but she slips inside the door, just to see. On the desk is the dummy of the first issue. Zoë walks carefully toward it. By now she's removed those foot-destroying boots and donned sneakers from her gym locker. Julia would be appalled, but Zoë doesn't care. Let Julia walk around with blisters all day.

Zoë picks up the dummy, feeling its weight. There must be twenty pages of her classmates' art and poetry. Her throat feels tight. Holding the soon-to-be magazine, she realizes how much it means to her, how much she wanted to be a part of the premiere issue. She remembers what Shannon said about how Zoë used to put her energy toward creative pursuits. The magazine is something she hoped to create. On the first page is a reproduction of someone's abstract painting, a chaotic mass of blues and reds. She opens it and sees a paragraph written by Sam:

Adults often complain about teenagers, saying we're self-absorbed, defiant, stubborn. We think we're at the center of the universe. But those people don't look closely enough. We're also human beings with imaginations, longings, hopes, and aspirations. See them here, in this first issue of Study Hall.

Zoë smiles. *Study Hall.* She likes the name. She likes the whole thing. She flips through the magazine, admiring the work Sam and the others chose. She reads the poems, losing herself, thinking about her own poems and how she would have liked to include a few. Only after she puts the dummy down does she think about the time. Her bus! She must have missed her bus. She grabs her bag and runs outside, but the buses are all gone. Worse, it's begun to rain, fat heavy drops, the kind that lead inevitably to a true downpour. She exhales, frustrated, and begins to walk. She can feel Julia's lacy top getting slowly soaked, her hair flattening against her head. Sure enough, the rain picks up speed, and soon Zoë is jumping over puddles forming on the sidewalk. Water streams from her hair into her eyes. A car beeps and pulls beside her. She turns to see Niles in the driver's seat of a beat-up old sedan. He leans over to roll down the passenger window.

"Need a ride?" he asks.

Zoë hops into the car, relieved.

"Where to?"

Zoë points him in the direction of her house. The windshield wipers beat rhythmically. She lowers the visor to look in the mirror and sees that her eye makeup has smeared halfway down her cheeks. "Great," she says as she tries to rub it off.

Niles glances at her. "You don't need to wear all that crap."

Zoë frowns. She never knows how to take what Niles says. Did he just pay her a compliment or is he being nasty? "Just focus on the road, student driver."

"Really," Niles continues. "You seem to be making a lot of effort for someone."

"It's none of your business," she says, smacking the visor back into place.

"I'm making it my business," he says, and smiles.

"You wouldn't understand." Trying to stay calm, Zoë watches the wipers go back and forth.

"Henry's done. You're wasting your time trying to get him back."

Zoë glares at Niles now, her heart hurting. "You wanted him to break up with me," she accuses him. "Why don't you just admit it?"

Niles turns and coasts to a stop in front of Zoë's house. "What are you talking about?"

"I know you called me Yoko. You wanted me gone." She hears that she's yelling.

Niles laughs. He and Henry have the same laugh.

They must have created it together, practicing until they got it right. "Henry called you Yoko too. We all did. It was a joke."

He smirks, his eyes on her. Zoë glares back, horrified and hurt. Henry made fun of her too? All this time she thought he cared for her, but he was laughing with his friends, calling her names.

"You're lying," she says.

"Alas," Niles says, that smirk still on his face, "I'm not."

"You are such an asshole," Zoë says, amazed.

"And you are a pain in the ass."

Then something surprising happens. Niles kisses her. He holds her wet hair in one of his hands. The wiper blades beat once, twice, again. And then he pulls back.

"Oh my god." Zoë puts a hand to her mouth, the mouth that was just kissed by Niles.

Niles doesn't say anything.

"What just happened?" Zoë asks.

He shakes his head. "You better get out."

Zoë gathers up her bag and opens the car door. She steps into the pouring rain. Immediately Niles takes off. Zoë watches as he does a quick k-point turn and heads onto Lincoln. The rain pounds on her head and shoulders as she walks to her door, still in shock. Inside, Logan is in the family room watching TV.

"Hi, booger," he says, and laughs at his joke.

Mom is in the dining room, hanging the completed curtains.

"Hi, honey," Mom yells. "How was your day?"

"Not great," Zoë yells back. She leaves her sopping sneakers near the door and goes upstairs to her room. She takes off the wet clothes and finds a pair of sweats and a tee. All the while, she tries to make sense of what just happened. She feels a pressure at her chest, but it's a different kind of pressure than she feels with Henry. It's not love. It's something else.

Then she knows what it is: it's opportunity.

She sits on her bed and lets herself think. Henry practically tripped over himself today when he saw her. She imagines him seeing Niles leaning in to kiss her, the surprise on his face, the outrage. The whole peeing on another guy's girl thing. Zoë closes her eyes. Plan B is taking off. Beautiful, brilliant Plan B is working. She calls Shannon.

"The eagle has landed," Zoë tells her. She starts to pace.

"What the hell are you talking about?"

"He kissed me."

"Who kissed you?"

"Niles."

She stops pacing and listens to Shannon gasp. "Whoa. Niles did? Really?"

"If I can time it so Henry sees, he'll come back to me. I just know it."

Zoë closes her door in case Mom can hear. She knows Mom would not approve of this scheming behavior, and she doesn't want anything to get in the way.

She's too excited. This is the thing that may finally work. She explains to Shannon her ideas for building on Plan B: go to open-mike night on the pretense of reading a poem, then kiss Niles in front of Henry.

"Are you sure you want to do this?" Shannon asks.

"Shannon!" Zoë is annoyed now. "You're the one who said I should use Niles. This is really your idea."

"I know, I know," Shannon says. "But now that it's actually happening, I feel funny. Like it's not fair to mess with Henry's heart like that."

"Not fair to mess with Henry's heart?" Zoë hears her voice rising. "You're worried about Henry's heart? With everything I've been through? With everything he's put me through? He used to make fun of me with Niles! Did you know that? And you're worried about his heart."

"You're right," Shannon says. "You're right. I'm sorry."

"Are you with me or against me here?"

"You know I'm with you. I'm always with you," Shannon says.

"Okay." Zoë takes a breath, trying to calm down. "Okay, good."

"Can I ask a question, though?" Shannon's voice is soft.

"Shoot."

"Why do you want him back so bad if he used to make fun of you? Doesn't that sort of make him an ass?"

Zoë puts her head in her free hand. Shannon's right.

But even so, even knowing this terrible thing, she can't seem to help how she feels. "I just do."

Later, as the rain pelts her window like drumrolls, and as she lies on her bed thinking about the fact that Henry teased her with his friends, Zoë concludes that it doesn't matter. She's lonely for him. She doesn't want to admit it, and she will not tell Shannon, but the truth is she wants him back simply to fill the space he left open. And if she can time things just right, if she can control the way it happens, she'll get Henry to see an impromptu kiss, a kiss that will turn everything around. A kiss that will change her destiny.

There's a knock at her door, and Mom peeks in.

"Just checking on you," she says. She's wearing a long, loose dress, and her hair is pulled back in a ponytail. Mom never wears makeup or slutty skirts. She doesn't have to.

"I'm okay," Zoë tells her, but Mom stays in the doorway.

"I can tell when my own daughter is lying to me."

Zoë sighs and rolls onto her side as Mom sits on the bed. Mom pushes the hair back from Zoë's eyes.

"Were you wearing makeup today?" she asks.

"Don't ask. It was a disastrous mistake."

Mom smiles and moves so she's leaning against Zoë's headboard. "This thing with Henry has really thrown you, hasn't it?"

"I guess."

"I know you don't believe me, but it will get better."

117

Zoë snorts. "Like you know anything about it."

"I know a little."

"You have Dad," Zoë says.

"My life didn't begin with your father, Zoë," Mom says.

Zoë watches her. Of course it didn't. She hasn't thought of this before.

"I had my share of failed relationships before Dad."

"You did?"

Mom nods.

"Why did I never know this?"

Mom shrugs. "It's nothing you needed to know before."

Zoë nods, encouraging her to tell more.

"I had a boyfriend in high school. We started dating my sophomore year. He was a junior. Black hair, blue eyes. He was a great kisser."

"Gross, Mom."

Mom smiles. "He was, though."

"Better than Dad?"

Mom narrows her eyes. "I'm not going to answer that question."

Zoë thinks briefly about Niles's kiss—a kiss that was pretty extraordinary, better perhaps than any of Henry's kisses—but she quickly shoos the thought away.

"He was different from other guys I knew," Mom continues. "He liked art. He played piano."

"A musician," Zoë says.

"Yup. We had so many conversations about things I

had never thought of before. The universe. Evolution. Our purpose here."

Zoë sees in Mom's eyes that she's far away, remembering. "Wow."

"I was always crazy with him, always worried he liked other girls or wasn't paying enough attention to me. I was a little like you've been behaving lately."

Zoë frowns. "Stick to the story."

"When he graduated, he broke up with me. He told me he didn't want to be tied down to anyone back home."

"Ouch."

"He broke my heart. I'd hoped we'd stay together and get married eventually."

"How terrible." Zoë touches Mom's arm. She knows what that's like.

"At the time I was sure there would never be anyone like him again. I was devastated."

"So, was there?" Zoë asks hopefully. This, she assumes, is the part when Mom will make her feel better.

"No."

Zoë widens her eyes, amazed. "Then why would you tell me this story?"

"There was never anyone else like him, Zoë, but there was your father."

"You still love the piano player!" Zoë exclaims, realizing what's going on.

Mom smiles. "I do in some ways. But the point is I found your father, whom I love even more."

Zoë nods, getting it. But she's still not completely satisfied. "Don't you wonder where Piano Guy is?"

Mom bites her lip. "I've thought about it at times."

"You should Google him." Zoë gets up and bounds toward her computer. "Let's Google him right now."

"No, Zoë." Mom laughs. "That's just it. I've moved on. I'm with your father, with you and Logan. I don't need to dredge up the past."

"But you do," Zoë says, emphatic. "You loved him."

"Oh, Zoë. You are so much like me."

Zoë looks back from her computer. "Name?"

"I get so focused like this too, pouring all my energy into something. With energy like ours it's too easy to lose sight of what's important. That's why I keep myself involved in projects that are actually productive."

"I'm guessing you're not going to tell me his name?"

Mom shakes her head and stands up. "But I am going to have you come down for dinner. And honey . . ." She pauses next to Zoë's desk. "Pay attention to what's important."

Zoë sighs. She knows Mom's right. She does get energized by single-minded pursuits and then forgets what matters most. But she also gets why she and Mom do that. When she's deep into something, she can't get stuck in the mucky stuff. She can keep moving forward and away.

Thinking about what Mom shared, Zoë feels a poem coming. She pulls out a piece of paper and jots it down.

We love who we love.
There's no planning, no
Decisions.
People come, they go.
You love them, you don't,
No matter what
they do for you.

She titles it "Piano Player, for My Mother" and slips it into her bag for later.

Day 18

Julia finds Zoë in the girls' bathroom.

"You're not dressed up!" Julia rebukes her. Julia's wearing ripped fishnets and a dress Zoë can only describe as revealing. A typical sort of outfit for Julia.

"I'm not doing it again," Zoë says. She fluffs up her unfluffable hair in the mirror. "It wasn't me."

Julia stands next to her and takes makeup out of her bag: eyeliner, mascara, blush, and lip gloss. Julia's parents don't let her wear makeup, so every day she puts it on when she gets to school. "But it worked on Niles,"

Julia says with a wicked smile. Obviously, Shannon called her.

"Keep it down," Zoë whispers. She looks under the stalls, making sure no one else is there. If word gets out about the kiss it could ruin her plan entirely. The point is for Henry to *see* her getting kissed by Niles, not *hear* about the kiss she and Niles already shared. And she definitely wants to witness Henry's reaction.

Julia puts a hand on her hip. "You didn't even call me."

"My mother came into my room, and then dinner . . ."

Julia looks at her doubtfully.

"I didn't want to make a big deal out of it."

"I need firsthand information," Julia says.

"Not here," Zoë says.

"No one's listening."

"Okay, we kissed."

"I heard that part."

"It was for like a second. There's nothing more to report."

Julia leans into the mirror to apply eyeliner. "No guy stands a chance against my boots."

"I wasn't even wearing your boots anymore." Zoë smiles despite herself. "I can't believe Niles actually kissed me."

"Who knew?" Julia steps back to examine her work, then moves on to mascara. "Niles has that whole I'm-too-good-for-you musician thing going on."

"You can't tell anyone, though," Zoë says, feeling

worried again. "I need to trust you and Shannon with this. It is essential that Henry see Niles kiss me." She tries some of the lip gloss.

Julia raises an eyebrow. "Uh-oh. Nothing good ever came of anything you started with 'It is essential that. . . .' "

"I don't know what you're talking about," Zoë says, although she most certainly does. There was her mother's fortieth birthday, when it was essential that they have forty-one candles on the cake (one for good luck), which led to the black spot on the kitchen ceiling. It was also essential that Shannon and Julia be the ones to try the results of Zoë's first foray into preparing Mexican food, which amounted to all three of them making emergency visits to the bathroom well into the night. "In any case," Zoë says, "keep your mouth zipped."

Two sophomore girls enter the bathroom. They look curiously at Zoë.

"Relax, girls," Julia says to them. "You got here too late to learn anything juicy."

They feign confusion and look away, as if actually minding their own business. Please.

Back out in the hall, Zoë and Julia collide with Madison.

"Hi," Madison says, swinging her hair like a horse's mane.

Zoë smiles. For the first time in a while, she doesn't mind seeing Madison with her ridiculously long blond hair and her perfect, full lips. Because Zoë believes she has a surefire plan to erase any girl but herself from Henry's mind.

As Madison walks out of view, Niles appears next to an exit door. Zoë senses a small somersault in her stomach. Not because she likes him, she reminds herself, but because he's the central figure in her plan. He's the front-seat passenger on this trip she's about to take. Julia nudges her.

"Are you going to talk to him?" Julia asks.

Zoë frowns. "You say that like I'm interested in him."

Julia shrugs. "You did kiss him."

"Shush!"

A few people twist around to try to hear what Zoë and Julia are saying, but Zoë ignores them.

"For your information," she tells Julia, "I am going to talk to him, but only to keep him interested until I can make my move."

Julia smirks. "Go to it, Dr. Evil." She gives Zoë a gentle shove.

Zoë goes to Niles and leans against the wall as nonchalantly as she can.

He turns to face her and grins. "Back to Keds, huh?"

"Listen," Zoë says, "we should probably talk."

He frowns. "About what?"

"About yesterday."

Some kids slow down as they walk by. Niles watches them. "Nothing happened yesterday," he says.

Zoë frowns. "Of course it did."

Niles looks away from her. He nods hello to someone.

Zoë can feel herself getting steamed. She hadn't considered Niles's feelings about the kiss. It was only a gateway to potentially getting Henry back. But now that Niles is suddenly denying it, she wants him to care. All of a sudden, *she* cares.

"I can't believe this," she says.

"Zoë, calm down."

"No," Zoë says, her voice rising. "I most certainly won't. Something *happened* between us, and you have the audacity, the arrogant audacity to—"

In one motion he grabs her arm, pushes the emergency exit door, and pulls her outside.

"Would you shut the hell up?" he says. "Do you want everyone to know?"

"Of course not," she says. "I didn't realize that's what—"

In the next second, his lips are on hers again.

"So does this mean that you *are* acknowledging what happened yesterday?" she says when they come up for air.

"Be quiet," he says, and kisses her a second time.

When they break free, Zoë says, "I always thought an alarm would go off if I went out the emergency exit. I always avoided it for that reason."

"Do you ever shut up?" He kisses her once more.

Later, she sits in English lit, dazed. Julia is behind her, unaware, doing the exercise they're supposed to be working on. Something about metaphors. Something that would be a breeze if Zoë could concentrate. But all she can think of is the kissing. The secret kisses outside the door. She puts a hand to her lips. Is she going insane? Is she actually developing feelings for Niles? Niles, who is also Henry's best friend? She shakes the thought away. That is impossible. She cannot—will not—do something as unbelievably stupid as fall for Niles.

She looks back at Julia, who is too busy writing to look up. If she can just make it to the next open mike, Zoë thinks, she will be saved.

Day 19

Niles strikes again. He catches Zoë off guard in the library and presses her against the biography stacks. His hands caress her shoulder, her hair, then slide down to her back. His lips are impossibly soft as he moves from her lips to her neck.

"Why are you doing this?" Zoë whispers when they stop to catch their breath.

Niles shrugs. "Why not?"

Day 20

Niles pushes Zoë into an unused stairwell.

Then into an unlocked janitor's closet.

"This is so bad," she breathes.

"So bad it's good," he whispers.

She can't argue.

She floats from class to class, trying to shake herself into reality, trying to stay focused. She can't let these feelings take over. But she finds herself looking for Niles, not Henry, always in anticipation of the next kiss. She squeezes her eyes shut. She has to stay on task, to surprise Henry with Niles's kiss. Plus she has Madison to contend with. And her friends—well, her friends don't exactly know about all this delicious, illicit kissing.

Day 21

By the time the weekend comes Zoë is so dizzy with feelings about Niles she decides to do something proactive. She goes to Madison's basketball game.

In the gymnasium she slides herself past the kids who attend games on a regular basis, the ones who shop exclusively at the Gap and wear ponytails every day (if a girl) or baseball caps (if a boy). They look at her oddly, curious about her presence. Zoë's never gone to see a varsity game in her life. She's not entirely sure why she's at this one either, except that she wants to keep an eye on her competition. She spots Madison with the other cheerleaders down on the floor. A few of them, Madison included, are stretching, lifting their legs high in the air like ballerinas. Show-offs.

As Zoë settles on the bleachers, she's surprised to see Sam coming toward her.

"What are you doing here?" she yells.

"I come to games all the time."

Zoë nudges the burly guy next to her so Sam can sit. "You do?"

"I'm a man of many wonders, a Renaissance man, an encyclopedia of sorts. You should take the time to get to know me. I won't disappoint."

Zoë laughs. Around her, people scream as the game starts up. "Go, Lincoln!" "Defense!" Sneakers squeak as the players run back and forth across the court, chasing the ball like eager dogs.

"The real question," Sam yells, "is what are *you* doing here?"

"I'm here to support Madison."

The guy next to her jumps up. "Yeah!" he yells. Zoë nearly leaps out of her skin.

"These people are animals," she says.

"Since when are you friends with Madison Pella?" Sam smiles, disbelieving.

As though she heard her name, Madison looks right at them. Zoë smiles hugely and waves. She adds a thumbs-up for good measure. Madison looks suspicious but returns the enthusiastic greeting.

"I'm a person of many wonders too," Zoë tells Sam.

Sam harrumphs. "I'm sure." When Zoë says nothing more, then stands to join a wave, Sam frowns. "What's really going on here?"

Zoë glances at him. "You're not buying this?"

"Not for a second."

"The truth is I'm doing recon."

"For what?"

"Madison is moving in on Henry. I'm here to learn more about her so I won't be blindsided." She watches as Madison jumps and kicks with the other cheerleaders. Her short skirt reveals how thin Madison is, which makes Zoë seethe. But then her mind starts to wander. A memory of Niles's lips on her neck. She shakes her head vigorously, getting herself back to the here and now. Madison. Henry.

Sam watches her. "You're a piece of work."

"But a smart piece of work," Zoë says, tapping her head, her eyes still on her rival. None of this would matter if Madison couldn't sing. Before Zoë knew about the singing, the cheerleading was enough to keep her from feeling worried. But Henry lives for music and Zoë isn't musical at all. It was always a wedge between them, probably the thing that made Henry split. She's determined to find a small flaw in Madison's perfect being.

"Why do you care so much?" Sam asks. "You're awesome."

Zoë sighs. "Madison is a singer. Henry loves music."

"So? You write poetry."

"Henry doesn't care about my poems."

"Maybe he would if you wrote the right one."

Zoë considers this. "I'm listening."

"Oh, no," Sam says. "I'm not helping you get your stoner boyfriend back."

"How many times do I have to tell you he's not a stoner?"

"Whatever he is, he's not the right guy for you."

Zoë watches him. "I thought you were mad at me."

Sam shrugs. "I'm not going to stay mad just because you're acting foolish. I know you. You'll come around."

"Thanks, Sam," Zoë says.

She watches the basketball players bounding around the court, the ball bouncing beneath hands, everything following a rhythm.

She stands.

"You're not staying?" Sam asks.

"It's really not my scene."

Sam shakes his head. "You baffle me, Zoë Gill."

"Join the club." Zoë gives his shoulder a quick squeeze.

She works her way to the end of the bleachers, tripping over knees, then climbs down the stairs to the exit. Madison watches her, clearly confused. One more member of the Baffled by Zoë Club.

• • •

The blank page glares at Zoë from her desk. Zoë has had a number of relationships with an empty screen.

Sometimes she loves it, the fresh possibility of a poem, and other times she abhors it. This is one of those other times. She stares back at the screen, at a loss. This can't just be any poem. This has to be *the* poem to end all poems. Because now she really will be reading something at open-mike night. And it has to make Henry fall at her feet with regret. This poem—along with Niles's kiss—has to single-handedly get Henry back. Like Sam said, maybe she just hasn't written the right one. She starts,

You make me better than I was before
Because before you I was . . .

She stops. What was she before Henry? According to Shannon, she was actually more dynamic. She was involved in literary activities and spent time with her friends. She was maybe more herself than when she was with Henry. She highlights what she wrote and deletes it. She doesn't want to think that way. She has to stay positive. Besides, hasn't she written more poems since D-Day than ever before? Henry has inspired her. She straightens her posture and tries again.

Without you I am better . . .

She holds the Backspace button. That didn't come out the way she intended. Once more:

You show me who I am.
I am a flower in your garden.

135

Longing for you, I grow and grow,
Waiting to be plucked.

She smiles. Now, that's a poem. She continues.

Remember that day on the beach?
You kissed me,
Setting off watery ripples
That stretched into the future,
Making me who I am.
That was the first kiss of 218.

She reads the poem a few times and, satisfied, prints it. Open-mike night, here she comes.

Day 22

Three dresses on hangers appear inside the dressing room.

"Try these on too," Julia says.

"Really?" Zoë holds them out, one by one, each more revealing than the last. Eighties new-wave music floats down from the ceiling.

"Do you want Henry and Niles to notice you?"

Zoë frowns but pulls a sleeveless red dress off its hanger and starts shimmying it over her body.

"What if I'm the only one dressed like this?"

"Sweetie, that's the point. You want to stand out Saturday night." Julia helps Zoë straighten the dress.

"You and Shannon will be there, right?"

"Are you kidding? We wouldn't miss it."

"And not just because you want to make fun of me?"

Julia smiles. "We're going because we're your friends."

Zoë zips the dress and turns to examine herself. "Wow!"

"You look amazing," Julia agrees.

After Zoë changes back into jeans, they rejoin the crowd in the store. Some girls are riffling through racks. Others stand in front of mirrors and hold pants up to their hips. The idea of all these girls wanting to look good, all the many girls in the world whom Henry might be with someday, makes Zoë feel insecure.

"Are you sure I should get this?" Zoë asks again. She imagines herself reading her poem, wearing this glamorous dress. The image is reassuring, but she has to admit that her plans don't generally go the way she pictures them.

"Of course you should," Julia says. She guides Zoë by the arm. At the checkout counter someone says her name, and Zoë turns around to see Madison with two of her cheerleader friends.

Zoë smiles. "Madison. What a nice surprise."

"Are you buying that?"

Zoë glances at the dress. She tries to press it into a little ball. "I'm thinking about it."

"Why do you care?" Julia steps between them. She puts her hands on her hips.

"I'm just asking," Madison says, "because I have the same one."

Julia glowers at her, while Madison keeps her gaze even. It really is incredible the amount of nerve Madison has for a freshman.

"I doubt that," Julia says. "This is from the summer collection. They just put these out this week."

Madison sneers. "My mother is a buyer at Saks. I get all my clothes before everyone else."

Julia glares at her a moment longer. Fashion is a sensitive issue for Julia.

"Nice seeing you, Zoë," Madison says, and walks away.

"Freshman bitch," Julia says under her breath, but just loudly enough so Madison will hear.

Zoë looks down at the dress. "I don't know," she says. "I better find something else."

"No freshman is going to decide your fashion fate." Julia grabs the wrinkled dress and throws it on the counter. It's the principle now. War. At least for Julia it is. "We'll take this," she tells the woman behind the counter.

At home, Zoë paces. She knows it's not a good thing when she paces. It means something is about to erupt. She doesn't know what happened. She was feeling so confident, especially after writing her latest poem. But now she has a sense of impending doom. She knows from her English lit books—when she used to read the books—that a sense of impending doom is most certainly not a good thing. She goes over her thoughts. She thinks she still loves

Henry. At the very least, she wants him to want her back. She's been kissing Niles. She's afraid she might possibly love him now too. In any case, she's hopeful that kissing him in front of Henry will spark waves of jealousy and desire in her ex-boyfriend. Something is terribly wrong with this picture, but she can't quite place what it is.

She calls Shannon.

"So don't do it," Shannon says.

"What? How could you say that?" Zoë sits to stop pacing, but now her right leg bounces. She presses on it to make it stop.

"If reading the poem doesn't feel like a good idea, then don't do it. It's no big deal."

"But, Shannon." Zoë chews at a hangnail. "This is my big chance. I have it perfectly orchestrated. First the kiss, then the poem. A double whammy."

Shannon sighs. "Then go."

"Why are you so unsupportive?"

"I'm sorry. It's just that this has been going on awhile, and I wish we could talk about something else."

"Forget it, then," Zoë says. "I won't talk to you anymore."

"I'm sorry, Zoë. I shouldn't have said that."

"No, I'm sorry I'm so boring." Zoë's aware that she has some nerve behaving like this, especially when she's kept the extent of everything that's happened with Niles from her friends.

"I just want you to focus on other things—more constructive things."

Zoë gets up to pace again, annoyed. "You always think you know what's best for everyone."

Shannon is quiet. Zoë knows she's hitting below the belt.

"I'm not one of your peer counseling students."

"What's your point, Zoë?"

"Just be there for me," Zoë says. "I don't see why that's so hard."

"But you just said you didn't know if you should—"

"Well, now I know I should."

Shannon is silent another moment. "Okay."

And with that, Zoë's resolve is once again strong.

Day 23

Zoë looks for Niles but doesn't find him. She wants one more make-out session to be sure Niles will be primed and ready for the kiss they'll present to Henry. It's irrelevant that Niles has no idea of her plan. At the start of the day, the kiss is a casual wanting, but as the day drags on, Zoë grows anxious. Each time she walks through the hallways she expects to be yanked into a stairwell or an empty classroom, but it doesn't happen.

"Where's Niles today?" she asks Shannon during lunch, trying to act as nonchalant as she can.

"Why would I know where Niles is?" Shannon smiles and Julia joins her.

Zoë shrugs. "I don't know. Just thought I'd ask, you know, in case you did know."

"You're so cute how you think you aren't obvious."

Zoë frowns. "I have no idea what you're talking about." She looks around the lunchroom, trying to seem like someone who really doesn't know what they're talking about, and who also doesn't care.

"Kind of a funny couple," Julia says to Shannon. "But if Zoë lasted that long with Henry, maybe it could work with Niles."

"Personally, I think she needs to take a break from boyfriends," Shannon says.

"What am I, invisible? I'm sitting right here!" Zoë yells. They look at her.

"Oh, really?" Julia says. "Because most of the time you're so caught up in your boy drama that you actually *don't* seem to be sitting right here."

"Damn," Shannon says. "That was harsh."

Zoë shoots Julia a look but doesn't say anything back because Julia's right.

Days 24-26

Niles still doesn't show, and without Niles around to kiss her, Zoë begins to doubt her ability to carry out her plan. She also finds herself missing the kisses themselves, although she is hard pressed to admit it.

By Thursday she's desperate enough about the Niles situation that she spends most of her free time sitting in a stall in the girls' bathroom, hoping to hear some information. Usually she hates Lincoln High's rumor mill, but for once it could serve a purpose. She is late to three classes and is pretty sure a new rumor has started suggesting that Zoë Gill has diarrhea. But by the end of the day she has learned the following: Niles has the flu, and a record label scout will be at the Big Top this weekend to hear Spaghetti Carbonara play.

Day 27

"Tomorrow's the big night, huh?" Sam comes up beside her as she makes her way to her bus.

Zoë frowns at him. "How did you know about Saturday night?"

Sam raises his eyebrows. "Need I explain?"

"Yes," Zoë says, pissed.

"Let's see." Sam looks up at the whitening sky to collect his thoughts. "Everyone knows some bigwig is going to the Big Top to see Spaghetti Carbonara. I saw you at the game last weekend, stirring up some plan concerning Henry and Madison. You raced off, and if I know Zoë Gill at all, it was to enact some part of that plan. And if I know you really well, it was to write a poem. I'm just putting two and two together. You're reading some lovelorn poem at the open mike, trying to get him to notice."

Zoë watches Sam with amazement. He grins, revealing his polished braces.

"You've learned way too much from the people at this school," she says.

"Perhaps."

"You really need a hobby, Sam."

He raises his eyebrows. "And you need to stop working so hard to get Henry's attention when I'm right here."

She smiles. "You're the one who needs to stop working so hard."

"Touché," Sam says.

On the bus ride home, Zoë's sense of dread deepens. She looks out the window at the grayish-white sky, signaling rain. She's terrified Sam's right. What if Henry isn't thinking about her? What if he's thinking only about the record label? He must be beside himself with excitement. This is what he's dreamed of, not reuniting with Zoë. Henry has been focused on his band since the beginning. For once, Zoë wants something in his life to be about her. Maybe her timing isn't the best, but she'll be damned if she'll go down without a fight. She's going to get the attention she deserved ever since they started dating.

At her stop she steps onto the sidewalk just as the first drops begin. Light, drizzly rain falls around her. She has the perfect dress, the perfect poem. Sure, she hasn't seen Niles in a week and has no idea if he's even thinking about her. Sure, Henry is going to be focused on Spaghetti Carbonara performing well for this scout. But she's not going to pull out now.

Day 28

On open-mike night, Zoë takes a breath and walks into the Big Top. Beside her are Shannon and Julia. She spots Henry and Niles, already onstage. Henry jams on his guitar. He swings his hair around, a signature Henry move. She never liked it. Too overdone rocker for Zoë's taste. Niles stands almost still, plucking on his bass and bouncing his head to the beat. In Zoë's purse is a copy of the poem. She smiles, feeling calm and purposeful, unafraid. Until she sees Madison. Wearing the same red dress. Zoë's heart rate jacks.

"That bitch," Julia says when she sees Madison.

"How did she know?" Zoë watches as Madison and her friends gather around a table near the front of the café.

"Ignore her," Shannon says. "Let's just find a table."

"But she's going to ruin my plan." Zoë can feel herself growing frantic. Shannon puts a hand on her arm.

"Zoë," she says, "try to have fun. You're going to kiss Niles, then read a poem. You're going to listen to some music. Hang out with your friends. This is all good stuff."

Zoë nods. "You're right." She takes a few breaths, doing her best not to think about Madison just ten feet away. "I'm going to put my name on the list and enjoy myself."

She makes her way to the front of the café where the band is playing. It is a song she knows. Henry wrote it; it's called "The One I Need." It isn't about her, of course. It's not about any girl. It's about some dog Henry had when he was a little kid. This always annoyed Zoë: he wrote a song for some dog but never thought to write a song for her. She watches Henry sing into the microphone, his voice smooth, and her chest aches. Even singing his stupid dog song, he destroys her.

She finds the sign-up sheet near the stage and writes "Zoë Gill, poetry reading." Feeling brave, she waves at Niles and winks. Niles startles and looks away. Henry, however, is now curious. He glances at Niles, then back at his guitar. "That's right," Zoë says aloud. "Be afraid. Be very afraid."

"Did you say something?" Now it's Zoë who startles. She turns to see Madison looking over her shoulder at the sign-up sheet. "Looks like you'll go on right after me."

Zoë stares at the sheet, horrified. Sure enough, there is Madison's name, written in rounded, looping script. There's a heart over the *i*. Zoë doesn't know how she missed it. "Are you going to sing?" Zoë asks, trying not to freak out.

"Uh-huh." Madison giggles, and Zoë considers using the pen attached to the sign-up sheet to pierce Madison's vocal cords. "I'm a little nervous, but I thought what the heck."

Zoë tries to smile. "Good luck," she says. As soon as Madison moves away Zoë crosses out the words *poetry reading*. Damn her! Zoë can't read a stupid poem after Madison belts out a song. She heard how good Madison is that day they came here. She presses the pen against her lip, thinking, thinking, trying to come up with something else to do. She looks up to see Henry swinging his hair, eyes closed, lost in his song, and it comes to her: she will dance. Henry liked her dancing. He thought it was sexy. She hasn't danced in half a year, but she can recall a routine she learned in jazz class. She writes *dance* beside her name and goes to find her friends.

She smiles as she approaches them. They bought three mochas with whipped cream. She doesn't have the heart to tell them she can't drink or eat anything right now. Her stomach churns.

"Sign up to read the poem?" Julia asks.

Zoë nods. She figures it's probably better not to tell them the truth. They'll probably try to talk her out of it.

"What about Niles? Do you have a plan for the kiss?"

Zoë glances back at the stage. "Not yet."

"I say you just go over and plant one on him," Julia says. She takes a sip of her mocha, leaving a whipped cream mustache.

"No," Shannon says. "You have to get *him* to kiss *you*. Otherwise Henry will think you're doing it purposely."

"She is doing it purposely," Julia says.

Shannon shrugs and makes a face that means *What are you gonna do when she's acting like an idiot?*

Annoyed, Zoë stands. "I'm going back over there."

Before her friends can say anything, Zoë walks away. There is an older guy, probably in his early twenties, sitting at a table near the stage. The scout. She walks past him, getting into sniper position: the side of the stage. How do you get a boy to kiss you? Acting on instinct, she looks directly at Niles and lifts one foot onto the platform. Then she leans over and pulls off her low-heeled shoe. She's not totally sure what to do next. Sexy is not really her thing. She rubs her foot as though it hurts. She doesn't get why feet are supposed to be alluring, but she knows they are. Niles sees her and, alarmed, turns away quickly.

"Ha!" Zoë says to no one.

"Zoë?" She jumps and turns to see Sam carrying a glass of water. "What are you doing?" he yells over Spaghetti Carbonara's loud music.

"Nothing." She smiles broadly and grabs the glass from him. She takes a few big gulps. "Just listening to the band."

He leans in near her ear. "Are you okay?"

"Of course!"

He gestures toward her bare foot. "Your shoe is off."

Zoë looks at her foot. "I think it's a bunion or something," she yells just as the music ends abruptly. A few people look over at her and then down at her foot. She slips the foot back into her shoe.

"Thanks for listening to us play," Henry says into the mike, looking right at the scout.

Perfect. Zoë eyes the band as they exit at the other side of the stage.

"Maybe you should sit and rest," Sam says.

Zoë waves her hand in the air dismissively. "You sit, though. I'll visit in a minute." She catches Sam's bewildered look, and from across the room she can see one of Shannon's feet tapping as she twists a dark curl, her signature move when she's frustrated. But Zoë can't worry about any of that right now. She has to stay focused. She marches over to where the band is huddling and stands before Niles. He tries to turn away from her, but she sidles around so she's in front of him.

"Can I talk to you a moment?" she says. She glances at Henry, who isn't missing a thing.

"Not now," Niles says. "We're busy."

"Just for a second," Zoë says. She tugs on his arm.

"Dude," he says, shrugging her off. "I said not now."

"I haven't seen you all week," she whines, knowing this will do it. Henry looks at them, confused, and Niles grabs her arm angrily and pulls her aside.

"What's the matter with you?" he growls. "You want Henry to know?"

Zoë bites her lip. "What if he did know? Would it be so bad?"

"Yes," Niles says. "Yes, it would be bad. You were Henry's girl. I don't need him pissed at me."

"Pissed at you?" Zoë's excited now. She's getting somewhere. "Why would he be pissed? Does he still like me?"

Niles grimaces. She stops. Wait, does Niles actually *like* her? "I have to get back to the band," he says. "We're in the middle of something."

"Stop." Zoë doesn't have time to think it through. She grabs him, hoping Henry's looking, and pulls Niles's face to hers. She kisses him deeply, his lips familiar now. She wraps her arms around his neck, holding him tight. But he doesn't return the kiss. He reaches for her arms, pulls them off his neck, and pushes her away. He glares at her fiercely. Anger? Hurt? Betrayal? She isn't sure. He heads to the bathrooms, and Zoë looks up to where Henry stands. Sure enough, he's looking. His face—oh, his face!—is filled with emotion. The same emotion she just saw on Niles's face.

In an instant, Zoë wonders what she's done.

This is when she hears the singing, Madison's singing. Madison's voice is so beautiful, so angelic and lovely, Zoë seriously thinks she might start to cry. But rather than cry, she does something else. Maybe it's the way Henry looks now, interested, watching Madison sing. Maybe it's the lingering feeling of Niles's lips and the fact that she will probably never feel them again. Maybe it's the way her friends are looking at her, like they pity her, like they have finally given up on helping. She's not sure what it is, actually, that makes her climb onto the stage. Madison's expression, midsong, contorts with outrage. She steps closer to the microphone, trying not to lose control of the moment. Without thinking, Zoë begins her dance routine. She slows it down, trying to make her moves match the rhythm of Madison's song. She thinks about how with their identical dresses this really does look planned. Any remaining shred of dignity Zoë possesses evaporates as she shimmies to the right and then to the left. Vaguely, she registers the faces she knows in the audience. Shannon, Julia, Sam, Henry. All four jaws drop. Shannon sinks her face into her hands, unable to watch. At least Niles is still in the bathroom. There is no question this was a bad idea. Zoë's face burns, her hands tremble, but it's too late. She has to finish the routine. She tries not to think about what will happen afterward, when Madison stops singing and

Zoë is done with her dance. She cannot imagine what she will do at that point. So she shakes her body through the moves, doing her best to make it good.

As she bends forward for the final pose, she hears her red dress rip up the back. At the same moment, Niles reappears, a look of utter shock on his face. That last shred of dignity Zoë had floats up into the air like a puff of smoke.

Madison finishes her song and stomps off the stage. Zoë slowly stands. Everyone is still watching, eyes wide, waiting to see what she will do. What else can she do? She bows, smiles, and walks sideways off the stage, holding her dress closed. Then she runs for the exit.

Day 29

Sunday. Done-day. Zoë lies in bed staring at her ceiling, contemplating how she will ever manage to leave her bed again. After a good twenty minutes she is decided: she won't. She will live out the rest of her days in her room. Her mother will bring meals in on a tray. They'll have to sponge her down and flip her every other day to avoid bedsores. Someone will videotape her classes and she'll send in her homework. Eventually she'll graduate, then work as a telemarketer, never having to get up. But suddenly she has to pee, and all her plans are ruined.

When she returns from the bathroom, Zoë gets a new perspective. She's already ruined her life. She's already embarrassed herself beyond any reparations. Why not go all the way? Why not just do this thing she needs to do? She dresses in jeans and an old sweatshirt. She throws her hair into a ponytail. She brushes her teeth and splashes some water on her face. And then she walks to Henry's.

She feels numb as she heads up the walkway to the front door and rings the doorbell. Numb as she watches Mrs. Bole hold the curtains back to see who it is, and as her face pinches with annoyance. The door opens and Zoë and Mrs. Bole stand facing each other. No more lies. No more manipulations. She's here to tell the truth this time.

"I need to see Henry."

"Henry just woke up, Zoë." Mrs. Bole stares down at her, surely fed up with Zoë's antics.

"I won't be long."

Mrs. Bole shakes her head. "Go home, Zoë," she says, but as she starts to close the door, Zoë stops it.

"Please," Zoë says. "It's not what you think. I'm here to apologize."

Mrs. Bole looks at her, unconvinced.

"I know I've done some stupid things this past month," Zoë says. "This is different. I promise you."

Mrs. Bole twists her mouth. Zoë can see how much she's messed up Mrs. Bole's view of her. Zoë's become something of a monster in her eyes. But then

Mrs. Bole says, "Okay, Zoë. But only if Henry wants to see you."

"Thank you." Zoë breathes out.

Mrs. Bole tells her to wait while she goes to get Henry. She closes the door, obviously not trusting Zoë with it open, and Zoë sits on the front stoop. She isn't sure what will happen. It's perfectly possible Mrs. Bole will come back to tell her Henry isn't interested in seeing her, which would be more than understandable, considering. She screwed up the night of his dreams. She stomped all over his heart, just like Shannon had predicted she would. And now she has the gall to show up at his house. But when the door opens again, Zoë turns and sees Henry standing there. It still happens when she sees him—that shock, that punch to the stomach. He still takes her breath away. He comes out and sits next to her. He's wearing sweatpants and his hair is messed—not in the way he purposely makes it look messy, but in a way that only happens when it's been slept on. It takes all of her to not reach out and smooth it down. They are both silent a few moments, watching the leaves of the tree she climbed shiver in the breeze.

"I can't believe you're showing your face here after last night," Henry says finally.

Zoë nods. "Last night was really regretful." She takes a deep breath, thinking how to start. She doesn't have a speech planned. As usual, she's acting on impulse, but there's no time to berate herself for that now.

"I don't have all day," he says. "If you have something to say, just say it."

"I'm sorry," she says. "That's what I came to tell you."

He looks down, quiet, so she figures she's off to a good start.

"Everything I did was about getting you back."

"Zoë—"

"I know I did it all wrong. You don't have to tell me that. But, just so you know, my intentions were always to win back your heart, and not to hurt you or screw up your life."

"You've been crazy, Zoë," he says.

"I know."

"Over-the-top crazy," he adds. "Boiling bunnies crazy."

"Okay, okay," she says. "I get it."

"You *danced* last night," he says.

She drops her head into her hands, mortified, and he laughs, and soon Zoë can't help laughing too. She and Henry haven't laughed together since he broke up with her.

"When you and I first went out, you had stuff going on," Henry says. "You were starting that literary magazine. You were a cool girl, Zoë. And then we went out and it's like you threw it all away to be with me."

Zoë stares at him, letting his words sink in. "That's why you broke up with me."

Henry meets her eyes. "I didn't want to be with

a chick whose only aspiration seemed to be to be with me."

Zoë shakes her head in disbelief and looks out at the street. "I can't believe what an idiot I am."

"It doesn't mean I stopped caring about you."

Zoë nods again, relieved to hear it. It also explains the look on his face last night. "I'm sorry I kissed Niles."

Henry winces, probably remembering.

"I shouldn't have done it."

"Forget it," he says.

"I hope you're not pissed at Niles."

He shakes his head. "Nah."

"If it's any consolation, I'm pretty sure he's never going to talk to me again."

Henry laughs. "That does sort of make me feel better."

Zoë laughs too, letting the knowledge that Henry cares whom she kisses wash over her. He doesn't want them to be together, for good reasons, but he still has feelings for her. That's a nice thing.

"I really did also want to focus on the band," Henry says. "I wasn't lying about that."

"What happened with that scout?" she asks.

"He gave us his card," he says, clearly excited.

Zoë smiles. She hates that she still feels jealous because the subject of the band makes him light up in a way he never did about her. "I'm happy for you."

"So are you going to lay off now?" he asks.

"I am."

He nods. She's not sure what he's thinking or how he feels. In some ways, she realizes, she doesn't know a lot about him. She was too focused on him liking her to get to know him, to *really* know him. She stands.

"I'll let you go," she says. She didn't mean to say something so significant, but she did. And now she's determined to stay true to her words.

● ● ●

When Zoë gets home, Mom is in the kitchen and Logan is in the family room, his gaze glued to cartoons.

"So?" Mom asks, bright and cheery. "How was last night?" She is regrouting the kitchen counter tile, her next project now that the curtains are done.

Zoë slumps into a chair at the table and rests her head on her arms. "Disastrous."

"Oh, no." Mom takes the orange juice out of the refrigerator and pours Zoë a glass. "It couldn't have been that bad."

"Did I say disastrous?" Zoë says. "I meant apocalyptic."

As though cued, the sounds of explosions come from the television in the other room. Mom sets the glass in front of Zoë, who takes a sip before hiding her head in her arms again.

"Do you want to talk about it?"

"If I do," Zoë says, "do you promise not to wince,

162

cringe, or otherwise make me feel worse than I already do?"

"Zoë." Mom laughs.

"Do you?" Zoë is quite serious. More explosions and gunfire from the TV.

Mom shakes her head. "You become more like your father every day. Yes, I promise." She puts one hand up as though swearing on a Bible.

Zoë tells her the whole story, everything from Plan B's inception and her first kiss with Niles to the horrific dance performance and her talk with Henry.

Afterward, Mom gets up, wordless. She hugs Zoë long and hard, then goes to put some bread into the toaster.

"Don't you have anything to say?" Zoë asks.

"What do you want me to say?"

"I want you to tell me how to make it better."

"I think you're already on that path." Mom turns and smiles at her. Zoë frowns. Mom is doing her usual you-know-what's-best-for-you routine. What Zoë really wants is some directions. A manual of some kind, filled with breakup rules. She's pretty sure, even if she hadn't behaved like a psycho for the past month, her heart would still feel like it had been dug out of her chest with a grapefruit spoon. So some guidelines would be nice.

Dad comes in through the back door from a jog.

"How are my lovely ladies this morning?" He goes behind Mom and she bends back her head for a kiss.

"And you?" He looks over at Zoë.

"I'm alive."

"She had a bad night," Mom says.

Dad laughs. "I'm scared to find out what that means." He gets a bottle of water from the fridge.

"Please," Zoë says. She stands and pushes her chair in. "Don't make me relive it yet again. Mom can fill you in."

Dad raises his eyebrows.

"Honey," Mom says as Zoë is about to leave the room. "I do have some words of wisdom if you're still in the market for them."

Zoë pauses. "I am."

"It may be too soon to see it this way, but maybe there's something to learn from all this, something you can take with you into your present relationships and relationships that have yet to be."

Zoë takes a deep breath and nods. She walks past Logan and the gunfire as she starts upstairs, but then decides to stop and turn back. She goes to the television and clicks it off.

"Hey!" Logan sits up, outraged. "I was watching that!"

Zoë mock-gasps. "It speaks."

Logan aims the remote at the TV, but she stands in the way of the signal.

"Mom!" Logan calls. "Zoë's bothering me."

"Zoë," Mom calls. "Leave your brother alone."

Zoë smiles and moves away, but just as her brother lifts the remote she jumps in front of the TV again.

"Move!" he yells. "Mom!"

Zoë laughs and walks off, letting him have his way. At least she engaged him in human conversation for a few moments. She heads up the stairs, knowing she's performed her first act in seven months of caring about something other than Henry.

Day 30

In the morning, when Zoë has to return to school, when she is quite certain Lincoln High will be alive with a colorful recounting of how she shamed herself in public, when she has to face her friends—if they are still her friends—she decides to first lie in bed and take a quick inventory of hearts. There's Henry's heart, which, just as Shannon feared, she obviously messed with; Niles's heart, also damaged; Sam's heart, always getting tromped on; Shannon's and Julia's hearts, belonging to two great friends who really did have her best interests in mind. Zoë had been cruel to Madison as well, ruining a truly awesome performance.

Then there's Zoë's own heart, small and hardened over these past twenty-nine days, still fiercely beating away. A heart that used to swell when she heard lines of poetry, that opened with joy when she laughed with her friends. A heart that poured out poem after poem, each expressing the particular colors and shapes she saw in her world. A heart that has spent the last seven months giving anything and everything to keep Henry, rather than paying attention to the things that kept it strong and whole. She puts a hand over the place where it resides in her chest. Today, she decides, is the end of the ending and the beginning of herself.

She gets ready for school. She puts on a cute sweater and jeans and sweeps her hair into a ponytail. She catches herself in the mirror. No makeup, no crazy hairdos or boots. Just Zoë. Good old Zoë. She smiles.

In the kitchen she downs a glass of juice, kisses Mom, ruffles Logan's hair. He says, "Don't touch me." She grabs her bag and goes out to meet her bus. She gazes out the bus window and remembers what Mom said about learning something from all of this. Beginning today, Zoë is determined to try to do what's right, and she knows she needs to start with her friends.

She finds Shannon first, outside Mr. Brown's classroom, and to her surprise, Shannon grabs and hugs her.

"I didn't think you'd be in school today," she says.

"You still want to be my friend?"

"Why wouldn't I?" Shannon looks concerned.

"Hello," Zoë says. "I'm the one who split her dress in front of a live audience the other night."

Shannon laughs. "That was pretty bad."

"Look at everyone," Zoë says, gesturing toward the students who are whispering and giggling as they pass by in the hallway. "Hanging around me will ruin your reputation." Right then, Madison walks past. She cuts her eyes at Zoë. Everything considered, she's still awfully bold for a freshman. But Zoë gives her her best look of apology, and Madison appears confused. She doesn't know what to do with this new Zoë.

Mr. Brown appears at the doorway. "Girls," he says. "Are we really going to have to go through this again?"

"Also," Zoë says quickly to Shannon, "I'm sorry. I've been a bad friend."

Shannon shrugs. Zoë knows that shrug. It means *You're speaking the truth, but I'd never say so.* "We'll talk later, okay?" Shannon says.

"Thank you," Zoë says.

In English lit Zoë writes a note to Julia.

Please say you're going to accept my apology.

When the note comes back to her she opens it.

That all depends on the terms.

Zoë writes back.

No terms, just undiluted gratitude for the best friends a girl could ask for. Do you accept?

Coming back, the paper flies past her, hitting John Lee on the head.

"What the—"

"John?" Ms. Carter gets up from her desk and walks over. She picks the folded paper off the floor. "Is this yours?"

Zoë looks back at Julia. "Nice," she mouths. Julia may be good at many things, but sports is not one of them. The whole class is poised, excited by this new turn of events.

"No," John says. He looks at Zoë, so Ms. Carter does too. "Ask Britney Spears over there," he adds, and while the whole class laughs, he high-fives the guy in the seat next to him. Zoë shrinks in her chair.

"Zoë?" Ms. Carter raises her eyebrows.

Zoë just shrugs, so Ms. Carter opens the paper and holds it at arm's length. "Don't get old, you guys. It sucks." She reads the note and looks at Zoë.

"Apparently, you've been forgiven," she tells Zoë. While the class chuckles, she wads the paper into a ball and drops it in the wastebasket. "And you'll need to see me after class."

Zoë frowns and glances back at Julia, who has joined in the laughter.

Great.

But seeing as this is the first day of the new Zoë, she decides to see getting in trouble as an opportunity. She really does need to speak with Ms. Carter about all her missed homework. The rest of her classmates leave, and before Julia too walks out, she says, "Think of it as karma for all your wrongdoings." Zoë stands as patiently as she can near Ms. Carter's desk.

"Zoë." Ms. Carter smiles and leans back in her chair. "Please tell me things are going to change sometime soon."

"I was just going to tell you they are."

"Really?" Ms. Carter looks doubtful. She presses her pen against her mouth. "What's happening with the boy? I'm assuming everything is still stemming from the boyfriend?"

"That's the thing, Ms. Carter," Zoë says. She holds her bag tight against her side. "I'm done with that. I'm moving on."

Ms. Carter's face brightens. "Someday you're going to look back and realize that this time in your life was just part of a larger, more enduring story."

Zoë nods. Most of her is internally cringing, knowing that Ms. Carter is about to start in with one of her poetic lectures on the meaning of life, but a small part is listening, maybe even eager to hear what Ms. Carter has to say.

"All of our lives have arcs, Zoë, just like in every good story. The many events that occur in our lives, good and bad, help build that arc. But what we learn from those events"—she points at Zoë to drive this last part home—"that is what makes the arc beautiful."

"Right," Zoë says, not sure she's understood a word Ms. Carter has said. She waits an appropriate amount of time, and when Ms. Carter doesn't say anything else, Zoë asks, "Is there a way I can make up the homework I missed?"

Ms. Carter thinks a moment. "If you do all the assignments, I'll grade them. I'll penalize for lateness, but you can still recover the grades."

"Thank you," Zoë says. Almost a month of homework to do. But it's like Julia said: karmic justice. Besides, what else is she going to do with her time now that she won't be scheming to get Henry back?

. . .

Lunchtime. No reason to dread it anymore. Zoë, Shannon, and Julia take their trays outside to their ledge and talk about the other night. Zoë finds herself laughing with them.

"You have no clue how to be sexy," Julia says. She turns to Shannon. "Did you see her rubbing her foot like she had some kind of rash?"

"You're really not helping," Zoë says, but she smiles.

This is when Niles walks by, his bass guitar in its carrying case slung over his shoulder. His mind seems elsewhere, until he sees Zoë. His expression changes, becoming guarded and hard.

"Niles," Zoë says. "Niles, wait."

But he walks on without looking back.

Zoë sighs, watching him go.

"There's probably something to learn from that too," Shannon says, always the peer counselor.

"I treated him like he wasn't even a person," Zoë says. "I so wish I could hit Rewind."

"I think he'll forgive you eventually," Julia says.

"I could have liked him if things had been different."

Shannon puts an arm around Zoë's shoulder. "You did like him, Z."

"Yeah," Zoë admits, leaning into Shannon's soft sweater, "I did."

• • •

After school, Zoë goes to the activity room. She sees Sam inside, along with a few other people. She takes a big cleansing breath and goes in. Everyone looks up.

"Zoë?" says one of the girls.

Sam looks back down at what he was doing.

"I'd like to work on the literary magazine again," Zoë says. "I hope that's okay."

"Of course it is," the girl says.

"Sam?" Zoë goes right up to him. "Is it okay with you?"

"You should do what you want to do," Sam says.

Zoë nods. "Is it too late to submit a poem?"

"We're past deadline for submissions," Sam says.

"Come on," the girl says. "It's Zoë. We can sneak another one in before we go to press."

Sam's expression hardens, but then he puts out a hand. "Let me see it."

Zoë opens her bag and gives him "Piano Player, for My Mother." He reads it quickly and passes it on to the girl.

"What a surprise," he says. "A poem about Henry."

"It's not about Henry," Zoë says, which is mostly true. "It's about my mother's boyfriend in high school. They broke up and now he's just a memory."

Sam leans against the table and crosses his arms.

"I'm sorry, Sam," Zoë tells him. "I really am."

Silence.

"I've been such a jerk."

More silence.

"I really hope you'll let me be your friend again."

Sam turns away and addresses the other girl. "We're going to have to reformat a bit to make room for Zoë's poem. See what you can do."

"Sam?" Zoë asks.

Finally, he gives her a break. "It's nice to have you back on the magazine," he says, and he walks away.

Zoë watches him go. It's not the reunion she hoped for, but it's a start. Probably the best she can get, considering. She has definitely learned something from the past month: her world doesn't always move at the pace she wants to set for it.

• • •

At home Zoë sits before her desk, working on calculus. She has a lot of catching up to do; it's hard to imagine how she'll do it all. But she has to. Just like her mother, she's decided to throw her crazy energy into productive activities.

But first she slips on her earphones, clicks on the radio, and lies back on her bed. This isn't so bad, she thinks as she looks up at her ceiling. All this time she was so anxiously trying to avoid being alone, with no one waiting on the other end of a phone, no date set up, no anticipation of kissing someone, no thinking about what some guy was thinking of her. But now here she is. Just herself. Zoë. Here on her bed listening to music.

The song she hears is yet another love song. It doesn't matter which one. *You're the only one for me, I can't live without you, you are my everything, I'm going to stay true to you.* For the first time Zoë sees how ridiculous and unattractive all this longing and clinging can be. She almost laughs. The answer seems so obvious suddenly, she doesn't know how she missed it. Just look inside, change it up. Stay true to *you*, not him. Of all the guidelines she needed during this past month, this is the one she realizes she needed the most. The one she should have written on her wall, should have licked and stuck to her forehead. *Stay true to you.*

That's what she's going to do.

Day 31

The next day Zoë sees him at the other end of the hall-way. Henry. That flippy thing happens in her stomach. She's not surprised. It may be that he'll always stir up that feeling in her. Perhaps she'll tell her daughter the story of their relationship, just like Mom told her about the piano player, to reassure her that it's okay to love someone and let go. Maybe this is what Ms. Carter was trying to tell her too.

Zoë calls Henry's name, and he looks over. She sees his first reaction—a grimace—which she supposes she deserves. But his next one is nice—a smile. They're friends now. Or at least they will be.

"Hi," Henry says, and this time his "Hi" doesn't pummel her.

She says it back: "Hi."

A few people stop to watch. *The Zoë-Henry Show* has become a favorite, and fellow students assume there's more good stuff to come. They don't know that Zoë has changed in the past few days, become more like the person she used to be. The one she liked. Because Henry did the right thing. By breaking up with her he helped her see that she had lost sight of herself.

They walk past each other, toward their classes, toward their separate lives. Zoë still feels sad but decides that's not the worst thing in the world. Their audience disperses, seeing that no sparks are going to fly. That's the thing about love, Zoë understands now. It feels exciting. It feels like the most momentous thing in the world. But really it's just another day on Earth. It's just something nice. It moves through the body, creating new divots and curves, preparing for the next love that will come through. And probably there is a next love, coming toward her this very minute.

She feels a poem coming on, so she drops to the floor—right there in the middle of the hallway, with all those people who have their own heartaches and lessons to learn stepping around her, unaware that something huge has happened, unaware that Zoë Gill has re-found herself right here on the floor of Lincoln High.

Acknowledgments

Thank you to Ethan Ellenberg and Françoise Bui. Thank you to Terri Brooks-Hernandez, Rebecca Grabill, and Bevin Cahill. Thank you to my truest loves, Michael, Ezra, and Griffin, who keep my heart plump and beating.

About the Author

Kerry Cohen Hoffmann's previous novels are
The Good Girl and *Easy,* an ALA-YALSA Quick Pick and a final-
ist for the Oregon Book Award. Kerry lives in Portland,
Oregon, with her husband and two sons. Learn more at
www.kerrycohenhoffmann.com.